# SUGAR
# & SPICE

OTHER BOOKS BY KEITH LEE JOHNSON
*Pretenses*
*Fate's Redemption*

# SUGAR
# & SPICE

## KEITH LEE JOHNSON

**SBI**

**STREBOR BOOKS**

NEW YORK  LONDON  TORONTO  SYDNEY

Published by

Strebor Books
P.O. Box 6505
Largo, MD 20792
http://www.streborbooks.com

Cover Design: www.mariondesigns.com

ISBN   0-7432-9610-9
LCCN 2003105030

First Strebor Books mass market paperback edition August 2006

10  9  8  7  6  5  4  3  2  1

Manufactured in the United States of America

For information regarding special discounts for bulk purchases,
please contact Simon & Schuster Special Sales at 1-800-456-6798
or business@simonandschuster.com

# ACKNOWLEDGMENTS

To HIM, who is able to do considerably more
than I can ask or think, I give thanks.

To my mother, thanks for always being
there for me.

To CHARMAINE PARKER, who did the final edit
on this work, thanks for the hard work you put
in. Thank you for taking all my calls, too.

EXTRA SPECIAL THANKS TO ZANE for taking
a chance on me. I appreciate your confidence
in my work.

To KUNG FU MASTER, JEFF WEASEL, who taught
me what little I know of the art. Thank you.

To MARTINA "TEE C" ROYAL of RAWSISTAZ
Book Club, thanks for spreading the word and
being a genuine source of encouragement.

To the dead (Bruce Lee, Malcolm X, Dr. Martin Luther King, Jr.), your words and philosophies live on in me.

Special thanks to Lauretta Pierce of the Literary World for the publicity.

Special thanks to the Toledo Public Library for all their help researching this and other projects.

To Sibylla Nash, thanks for all the insight and a myriad of helpful questions.

To Rush Limbaugh, you once said people should invest in themselves. I heard you, dude, and did just that. Thank you!

Special thanks to Billie Kwiatkowski, Gail Washington, and other former co-workers, who read the work and made suggestions while this book was still being written.

# PROLOGUE

THE TWINS WERE FREE!

After ten long distressed years of confinement in two of the nation's worst prisons, the twins walked to a waiting black stretch Lincoln limousine without looking back at the gray cement fifty-foot walls that had imprisoned them. It was an experience far from the life they had known—a life of privilege and ease—a life given to them by rich absentee parents. In prison, however, they were just another pair of inmates with numbers stenciled to their dungarees.

Norrell Prison was full of corrupt officers who, following the lead of the warden, were as depraved as the criminals they guarded. Many of the officers were taking payoffs from the gang leaders who were heavily into the drug trade, smuggling in heroin, marijuana, and crack cocaine. But the most detestable crime the correctional officers allowed was the buying and selling of inmates. Sexual predators ran rampant in the prison, gang raping the weaker prisoners. It was gladiator school 101.

The most nauseating aspect of the widespread corruption was that the prison ran smoothly with the free flow of drugs and limited anarchy. Restricted depravity kept the prisoners from rioting and murdering each other at will.

Initially, the twins were offered protection from the sexual predators if they would give sexual favors to just one inmate. They refused and were subsequently attacked by several career criminals. Fighting back earned them thirty days of solitary confinement.

At first, they complained to the warden but that only invited reprisals from the inmates and guards. They tried to escape and had their sentences lengthened by six years. Soon, they learned to play the game and bided their time. To survive, the twins became compliant and gave into the debauchery. They had been bought and sold like chattel on an auction block. Every orifice became an instrument of sexual pleasure.

As the years passed, the twins became stronger mentally and physically. They began to build their slender bodies, turning them into muscular walls of stone. They challenged each other nightly in their cell to see who could do the most pushups. After five years of nightly challenges, they were able to pump out five hundred.

By the time they could do two-hundred pushups, they realized they were stronger than the prisoners and guards who had molested them, but they needed to endure—needed to stay in control—needed to stay alive. They continued to indulge in the wanton debauchery, knowing that in time, they would be free.

With two years left on their sentences, the twins were viewed as model prisoners and were given comfortable jobs in the library where they had access to the computer systems. The assignment afforded them plenty of free time to plan and scheme.

Every night, in their cell, they talked until the wee hours of the morning, choreographing every murder. Revenge was going to be so sweet—served so very cold. Now they were free!

# CHAPTER 1

The palm trees, the sunshine, and the gracious amenities of the hotel were a welcome diversion from my rigorous duties as FBI Agent Phoenix Perry. Just a few weeks ago, I had killed Coco Nimburu, the cunning assassin who had terrorized Washington, D.C. She had killed my father, kidnapped my family, and even hospitalized Kelly McPherson—my partner. A family vacation in California was just what we needed.

We had begun our family excursion in San Francisco. Kelly and I were there last month investigating the Warren family murders—more of Coco Nimburu's handiwork. She had killed twelve FBI agents, chopping the heads off two of them before killing Mr. and Mrs. Warren.

Having been in the city by the bay again made me want to take Savannah there for her first real vacation. San Francisco was the first city I had visited when my father and I returned to the United States.

My father had been in Naval Intelligence—assigned to the American Embassy in China for twelve years. I, however, spent most of my twelve years studying the martial arts under the tutelage of legendary Kung Fu Master, Ying Ming Lo.

After taking in as many of the sights as we could get in for the five days we were in San Francisco, we flew down to the City of Angels. Coco Nimburu had entrusted her remains to me. She had harbored a secret desire to be an actress and asked me to sprinkle her cremated remains on the Paramount Studios lot, which was no easy task. I had to take several tours to accomplish this, sprinkling a little of her all over the lot. The important thing was that I had done as she had asked and that made me feel good. Even with all that she had done to my family and my circle of friends, I had felt a kinship with her and missed her mind games and her infectious laughter.

I was sitting in the Café Sierra restaurant, reading the complimentary copy of the *USA Today*, waiting for my husband and daughter to join me. The warden of Norrell Prison had been murdered back home near Washington, D.C. According to the paper, Mr. and Mrs. Louis Perkins had been brutally killed in their home. They had both been savagely lashed with a whip. The killer had raped the wife repeatedly throughout the night, then dismembered her and her husband with a chain saw. Large amounts of cocaine and money were found near their decomposing corpses. They had been dead for a week. Captain Callahan, who ran the prison, told a reporter that Warden Perkins was supposed to be vacationing in the Cayman Islands.

Just as I finished the article, Keyth and Savannah came to the table and sat down. I looked up from the paper at my husband and shook my head. He had been an FBI agent and instantly knew that something terrible must have happened. I gave him the paper and he began reading it.

"Hi, honey," I said to my daughter. "You ready to go to the park?"

"Yeah, Mommy." Savannah beamed.

I had promised her that our first stop today would be the *Terminator T2:3D* theater at the Universal Theme Park. We had seen the exciting short film once and Savannah wanted to see it again, but the lines had looked like a two-hundred-yard anaconda. We were flying back to Washington tomorrow afternoon and this would be our last chance to see the Arnold Schwarzenegger, Linda Hamilton, and Edward Furlong look-a-likes being chased through the theater by futuristic terminators, with loud explosions and laser fire all around us. It's truly an unforgettable experience. Truth be told, I was just as excited as my daughter.

# CHAPTER 2

The twins watched Heather Connelly drive a silver Bentley Arnage down the long winding driveway, then through an electronically controlled gate. She stopped briefly, looked both ways, and turned right onto Pacific Coast Highway. After starting a yellow Hummer, they followed her.

Heather Connelly was twenty-seven years old, tall, slender and tanned, with brunette shoulder-length hair. The vivacious beauty had won the Miss California crown at eighteen. She had hoped to win the Miss America title and perhaps go on to win the Ms. Universe pageant but was sidetracked by a bout with cocaine that derailed her chances of winning and threatened her looks.

Heather Connelly had been Malibu High School's most promising pupil. She was class president, valedictorian, prom queen, and president of the National Honor Society. Her musical talents included playing piano, saxophone, and violin. She also had a powerful singing voice before her bout with cocaine. Like Christina Aguilera, Heather could sing pop, jazz, and rhythm and blues, but she preferred opera.

Today marked the fifth year that Heather Connelly had been clean and sober. It was a time for celebration. She wanted to show Jasper Hunter, the man who had helped her beat the cocaine addiction, just how grateful she was. Tonight she planned to fulfill a particular fantasy of his, but she needed something special for the romantic interlude.

Jasper Hunter had been a counselor at the Wise Counseling Center in San Francisco when he and Heather met. He had found her extremely attractive, but dating the clientele was grounds for dismissal. He ignored the rules like he had so many times before and fell under Heather's intoxicating spell. William Wise, the owner, discovered them in a compromising situation and fired Jasper on the spot. By that time, Heather was well on her way to conquering the addiction that had gripped her very soul.

The twins followed Heather at a distance down Pacific Coast Highway, discussing whether they should use the bumper on the Hummer to push her off the cliff into the Pacific Ocean. Having something better in store, they decided not to.

Heather Connelly turned into the parking lot of the Pier View Café and backed the Bentley into an open space between a black Porsche Carrera GT and a fire-engine red convertible Lamborghini Diablo near the canopy entrance of the restaurant. She planned to have brunch with Sandra Rhodes and Paula Stevens, her loyal Malibu High School friends. Heather got out of her car and strolled into the restaurant. She was wearing a white, oversized, V-neck sweater and lavender spandex leggings that showed off her long shapely legs.

The twins parked the Hummer several rows away from Heather's Bentley and watched her float into the café as if the world were hers to do with as she pleased. With high-powered binoculars, they could see Heather approach Sandra and Paula who were waiting for her on the deck. They watched the women talk for about an hour, sipping cool beverages from tall hand-painted margarita glasses and eating jumbo shrimp. On occasion, the women laughed and slapped high-fives.

"Look at them, Sam!" Alex blared in the Hummer. "Greedy bitches!"

"Let 'em enjoy their little meeting," Sam hissed. "It'll be their last."

# CHAPTER 3

**B** *reast implants* were the words that ran though the minds of the twins as they looked attentively at the statuesque women. With the exception of their enlarged bosoms, all three women looked virtually the same as the twins remembered—better in fact. It was clear that they had kept themselves in shape, probably on one of the stairmasters at the Malibu Health Spa.

After about an hour and a half, Heather Connelly, Sandra Rhodes, and Paula Stevens left the Pier View Café. Sandra drove the Diablo. Paula drove the Carrera GT. No doubt about it, all three women had done well for themselves over the past ten years. They zipped out of the parking lot like three adolescent males trying to prove their manhood and raced down the Pacific Coast Highway. Sandra and Paula headed toward home, but Heather went on to Santa Monica.

Less than thirty minutes later, Heather Connelly

had reached the Santa Monica Mall, where she searched diligently for the perfect lingerie that would set Jasper Hunter's heart aflame. After scouring Neiman Marcus and Dillards, she finally settled on a red silk teddy with a plunging neckline, matching fishnet stockings, garter belt, and stockings from Victoria's Secret.

Having found the seductive garments, Heather drove back to Malibu with Destiny's Child's "Independent Women" blasting in the CD player, still unaware of the yellow Hummer that followed at a distance.

Heather sang along with the Grammy-winning trio: *"Lucy Liu...with my girl Drew...Cameron D and Destiny...Charlie's Angels come on."*

It was almost six-thirty when she pulled up to the gate. The power window hummed as it slid down. After hitting the appropriate numbers on the keypad, the gate swung open and she drove up to the secluded French Normandy mansion that boasted a thirteen-car garage and parked the Bentley.

The twins waited for what they thought was sufficient time for Heather to park the car and enter the house, then drove up to the gate. They knew the code. The gate opened and they drove in undetected.

# CHAPTER 4

The twins parked the yellow Hummer in the garage. With backpacks strapped on, they followed the paved trail that led to the white solid oak French doors of the mansion. After shutting off the alarm, they entered the multimillion-dollar residence with a key that had been given to them.

Heather hadn't bothered to change the locks or alarm codes in the ten years that the twins had been away. It wouldn't have mattered even if she had changed the codes. The twins were prepared. Thanks to the Internet, they were able to find and purchase an electronic device that was capable of finding the code to virtually any alarm system.

The Connelly mansion was exactly as they had remembered it. A familiar scent filled the air. Heather always burned jasmine incense when she made love, the twins remembered. Standing in the foyer, they looked at the white painted walls, the black and white marbled floor, and the crystal chandelier that hung above the split stairway that led to the bedrooms.

Quietly, they walked up the carpeted staircase to look for Heather. They knew her habits. She didn't spend over three and a half hours shopping for a silk teddy for nothing. She was expecting a man to come over later. By now, Heather was taking a bath, washing the day's dirt off her sculptured body. Or relaxing in the sunken tub as the mini-jets massaged every part of her.

As the twins approached the top of the staircase, they heard Heather's unmistakable sighs. They were familiar with her distinctive sounds because they had heard them many times before. Stealthily they crept to the open door of the master bedroom where they watched Heather and a man they had never seen before making love.

Heather was on top of the man, riding him at a fiery gallop, writhing with tight twisting motions that drove the man wild. The sight of their passionate lovemaking threatened to ignite the twins' lustful appetites and set them ablaze. Just as their corporeal urges began to kindle, Heather sighed loudly, fell forward, and panted heavily. The twins leaned against the hallway walls and listened to them.

"Jasper," Heather began in soft intimate tones, "I

talked to Sandra and Paula at the café and they agreed to a foursome tonight; if you still want it."

"Really?" he asked skeptically, but also excited.

"Yeah. They're coming by later tonight."

# CHAPTER 5

After hearing that, the twins smiled, then tiptoed back down the hallway, back down the staircase and out of the house. This was better than what they had planned. Now they could kill them all at the same time. At a brisk pace, they followed the paved trail to the back of the mansion and down the stairs, past the swimming pool, past the tennis courts to the guesthouse to wait for Sandra Rhodes and Paula Stevens.

Being in the guesthouse again triggered a bit of nostalgia for the twins. It was there that they had met Heather, Sandra, and Paula at a swimming party the Connellys had thrown for their daughter. Almost all of Malibu High had attended the teen shindig.

Reminiscing, the twins could almost hear the screams of young teenage bikini-clad girls who had been pushed into the crystal blue pool. Cameo's "Word Up" had been blasted repeatedly that day. They could even smell the catered Mister Big Stuff

Plantation Barbecue. They could almost taste the succulent meat and the accompanying special sauce that separated Mister Big Stuff's barbecue from all others.

Their anger began to swell when they thought about what had been taken from them. They had missed Malibu and everything about it. Late at night, in their cell, they pretended to be on the beach basking in the glow of the Malibu sun. Remembering the hot summer days and cool nights were a welcome getaway from the brutal realities of prison. But now, they had to focus on the task at hand. In a few hours, Paula and Sandra were coming to the Connelly mansion and then the fun would begin.

Alex pulled out the high-powered binoculars and looked at the master bedroom. The mansion was full of picture windows and the couple would be easy to spot. For a moment, Alex wondered if Heather and her friend had seen them scamper down the paved trail to the guesthouse, then dismissed it. A few seconds later, Heather and the man in her life were spotted getting into the Jacuzzi in the raw. The twins decided to relax, too. They had waited ten years. They could wait a few more hours for Paula and Sandra to arrive.

# CHAPTER 6

L ooking in the mirror, I could still see some of the dark bruise from the broken jaw I had sustained last month. I had been in a barroom brawl at a jook joint called The Spot in Lower Manhattan. I picked up my toothbrush and dabbed it with some Colgate gel before putting it into my mouth.

The vestiges of After 7's "Ready or Not" played softly on the clock radio when I turned it on. I loved that song. While I brushed my teeth, I thought about the murdered warden and his wife. I knew I was on vacation, but I was still an FBI agent and the murders had puzzled me the entire day. The piece in *USA Today* led me to believe that the warden and his wife were killed for personal reasons. Otherwise, why leave the drugs? And more importantly, why leave the money? The killer must have wanted the authorities to know that the warden was involved in the drug trade. That was the only thing that made sense to me.

"How long you gon' be in here?" I heard my husband ask me.

I could see his image in the mirror. He was leaning against the opening of the bathroom, wearing a pair of navy briefs that hugged his tight loins.

"Not long," I said after spitting out the used Colgate.

"You thinkin' about those D.C. murders?" he asked. It seemed to be more of a statement than a question.

"Yeah," I answered. "Have you given it much thought?"

"Some, but not much. I'm on vacation," he said sarcastically.

I stopped brushing for a second and looked into his brown eyes to see if he was angry with me. He folded his massive arms and a smile emerged. One of the things that bothered him were all the hours I spent working my cases. You would think he'd understand, having been an agent himself. But it's like that when you're a woman. Men expect everything from you, regardless of your chosen vocation.

"We're going back to Washington tomorrow. Our vacation is just about over. So please don't give me attitude, hear?"

"You ready to get back to work, huh?"

"Yes," I told him. "Too much vacation can wear a sista out."

"Savannah's asleep," he said.

My husband was telling me that he expected to get some on our last night before going home. And there was no way I was going to get out of it, not that I wanted to. I smiled at him, and then spit the residual toothpaste into the basin. Keyth walked up behind me and rubbed himself against me. I wiped my mouth and smiled again.

# CHAPTER 7

I squeezed the bulge in his shorts after turning around and facing my husband. He put his arms around me and we kissed softly. Our lips made a smacking sound when we pulled away.

"You think the way they were killed was a message, don't you?" Keyth asked.

"Either that, or it was personal," I answered. "A message or not, it's weird for someone to kill that brutally and leave drug money at the scene."

"Yeah, it was weird. Kinda rules out a former prisoner, doesn't it?" Keyth asked.

"I tend to agree with that, honey. But who the hell knows these days? They could have left it to let the police know that the warden and his wife were involved in criminal activity. Or they could have left it to fool the police into believing that an ex-con had nothing to do with it."

"So you think that a former prisoner did it and left the money to cover his ass, believing that the police would never believe an ex-con would leave the drugs and money that could have easily been taken?"

"It's possible, but I doubt it," I said. "To tell you the truth, Keyth, I have a hard time believing that any convict would leave money and drugs there when they could have gotten away clean."

"Yeah, me too. If I were running the investigation, I would still start at the prison, wouldn't you?"

"Probably, but if the warden was in fact buying and selling drugs, someone on the street would know about it. Someone on the street had to be moving the stuff for him, assuming of course that he was involved in the drug trade."

"So then, you think it was about drugs?" Keyth asked again.

"I think it was personal, no matter who was involved. Whipping them makes that clear. Plus, I just don't see drug dealers leaving the drugs and money there."

"What if they were in a hurry, Phoenix?"

"Why would they be, Keyth? According to the paper, the victims had been dead for about a week, which means the killers had plenty of time. And on top of that, it took some time to dismember them. No, he wasn't in a hurry. The killer took his time. And what about raping the wife? Would a drug dealer

rape the wife and leave the money? That's been bug-
gin' me all day."

"Speaking of taking his time." Keyth smiled. "I
plan to take my time, too."

# CHAPTER 8

My body trembled at my husband's touch. We were still in the bathroom, still standing, still facing the mirror. My eyes were closed. Keyth's hand was inside my panties, moving slowly—deliberately. His fingers found my sensitive areas with ease. With his other hand, he massaged one of my nipples through my bra. I couldn't resist, even if I had wanted to. I was putty in his hands. We had been married for eight years and our sex life was still incredible. I felt myself starting to sway rhythmically as the pleasure he gave me began to mount.

I opened my eyes and saw him watching me voyeuristically. I could tell that the pleasure he gave me somehow stimulated him. I closed my eyes again, which seemed to enhance what I was feeling.

"Just like that," I heard myself saying.

Moments later, my legs started to shudder as I approached orgasm. I could feel my husband's hardness pressing against my back, threatening to puncture my skin. Even though Keyth initiated the sex, I needed it also. I was almost there...almost there.

"Yes...yes...yesssssssssss!" I shuddered.

That was all Keyth needed to hear. I swear two seconds hadn't passed before we were on the bathroom floor, thrusting our pelvises relentlessly, moaning and groaning like animals in heat. The floor was hard, but I didn't care. My body demanded pleasure and I gave into it. Our bodies slammed hard against each other in perfect harmony until we climaxed together.

We lay there on the floor, catching our breath. Keyth's head was on my chest and I stroked his hair gently as we listened to Billy Preston's "With You, I'm Born Again." Keyth had dedicated that song to me at our wedding reception.

"You remember this song?" I asked him.

"Uh-huh," he said in a low semi-conscious voice.

I laughed. I could tell he was on his way to Never-Never Land. It had been a long day. We had been at the Universal Theme Park from the time it opened at eight a.m. until eight p.m. and he was tired.

We had lunch at the Hard Rock Café, which was full of Hollywood legend look-a-likes. Our server was Sidney Poitier. Rarely do I allow my daughter to eat junk food, but today I let her have whatever she wanted. We ate Buddy Holly burgers, French fries, and Haagen-Dazs ice cream.

After we finished eating, Savannah dragged us to the *Back to the Future* ride, Steven Spielberg's *Jurassic Park*, Ron Howard's *Backdraft*, Kevin Costner's *Waterworld*, James Cameron's *Terminator 2:3D* and everything else in the park. It had been hot and the lines were long. We baked in the sun for at least an hour and a half at each ride. But Savannah loved it and that's all that mattered.

# CHAPTER 9

Loud music blared from the Connelly mansion, awakening the twins who had fallen asleep in the guesthouse. After a few seconds, they recognized the tune. It was Levert's "Casanova." Evidently, the party was underway. According to the digital clock resting on the fireplace mantle, it was a little after eleven. Alex picked up the high-powered binoculars and looked through the lenses toward the mansion. It looked like every light in the house was on. Alex could see Heather, Sandra, and Paula in the recreation room on the first floor.

The man that Heather had had sex with earlier was sitting in a chair, watching Paula peel off her clothing. Sandra, the natural blonde, was leaning against the eight-foot pool table watching the show. She was wearing a leopard jacket and a short black skirt that barely covered her derriere.

"You ready, Sam?" Alex asked.

"Yeah, let's go."

They grabbed their backpacks, put on a pair of surgical gloves, and walked out the door. It was dark outside, but they found their way back easily by following the paved trail past the tennis courts, past the swimming pool, and up the stairs. Suddenly the music stopped. By the time the twins finished climbing the stairs, Heather and Sandra were locked in a vise-like kiss near the pool table, ripping at each other's clothes. Paula, completely nude, was on her knees in front of the man sitting in the chair. Her head bobbed up and down rapidly like a crack whore who had been promised a vial full of the addicting drug.

The twins walked around to the front of the house. They wanted the element of surprise. When they reached the front of the mansion, they saw the red Diablo and the black Carrera GT parked in the circular driveway. Alex turned off the alarm and they entered the house undetected again. Their hearts began to pound the moment they entered the residence.

"This is going to be absolutely delicious," Alex whispered.

"I know," Sam whispered.

# CHAPTER 10

S lowly, so as not to draw attention to themselves, the twins unzipped the backpacks and
pulled out an Omega stun baton that was
guaranteed to make even the fiercest assailant
behave. The baton had one hundred fifty-thousand
volts running up and down the entire unit above
the handle. Any part of the baton would render an
assailant unconscious. They tiptoed down the hallway past the living room, through the kitchen, and
past the formal dining room.

As they approached the recreation room, they
could hear the sound of raw sex emanating from the
room. The sound was so distinct—so animalistic—
so erotic that it aroused the twins. With their backs
against the wall, they peered around the opening
and saw Heather Connelly's face buried in Sandra
Rhodes' blonde crotch. Sandra's black skirt was
pushed up over her butt, her feet flat on the table with
her legs at a forty-five-degree angle. Her surgically

enlarged breasts were exposed and her leopard panties dangled on her right ankle.

The man and Paula were on the floor facing the pool in a doggy-style position. He was thrusting in what looked like an angry fury. Paula's sighs were high-pitched and rhythmic. She twisted her long neck so that she could look back at the man. Paula was a very pretty brunette with dimples and thick black arched eyebrows. Her hair was short and curled to the back.

The twins waited until Paula faced the pool again before entering the room. The couples were so absorbed in their eroticism that they had no idea the twins were there. They walked over to the bar and poured a glass of chilled chardonnay. They sat down, ate a few shrimp, some cheese and crackers, and watched the show. After a few more voyeuristic minutes, they walked over to the man and Paula.

"Having fun, kids?" Alex laughed, and lifted a champagne glass as if a toast was being offered.

The scene immediately switched from one of rampant sexual abandon to that of a deer being caught in the headlights of an oncoming car. The moaning ceased and the man pulled out of Paula. With the exception of Heather, they all scrambled to find their clothes.

"Who the hell are you?" the man asked.

"Don't worry about it," Alex told him and zapped him with the baton. Paula was about to say something and Alex zapped her also. Both of them were unconscious.

Alex walked over to the bar, picked up a towel and then walked over to Heather and threw it in her face.

"Wipe her juice off your mouth!" Alex demanded.

# CHAPTER 11

"Why? You've tasted Sandra already!" Heather shouted back.

Alex backhanded Heather. "Wipe-your-mouth," Alex repeated through clenched teeth.

Heather reluctantly wiped her face. When she finished, Alex kissed her hard on the mouth. "Did you miss me, baby?" Alex asked.

Sandra had finally put her panties back on and covered her breasts. She was about to say something when Alex zapped her with the baton. She fell to the floor.

Heather frowned. "What did you have to do that for, Alex?"

Alex backhanded her again. "You don't ask me questions! I ask you questions!" Alex told her and slapped her three more times—first with a backhand, then a forehand, then a backhand again. "You got that?"

Heather nodded. Alex zapped her with the baton and she fell to the floor.

"Alex, let's get rid of the guy first," Sam suggested. "He wasn't supposed to be a part of this. But, he's seen us. He knows what we look like. He's gotta go. The sooner the better."

"How do you wanna do it, Sam?"

"Let's take his ass out back and toss him over the cliff," Sam said. "First, we better make sure the women are here when we come back."

Alex pulled several plastic zip-lock straps and tape from the backpack and tied the hands and feet of the women so they couldn't escape—then taped their mouths shut. They tied up the man, and then one by one, the twins carried Heather Connelly, Sandra Rhodes, and Paula Stevens upstairs to the master bedroom.

When they came back downstairs, the chardonnay was taken out of the bucket of ice and placed on the bar. Alex grabbed the bucket of ice and they took the man out to the bluffs. Alex tossed the melted ice water into the man's face and he came around. The shock of the freezing cold water snapped him out of it.

"Hey! What the fuck is going on?" the man shouted.

"You were in the wrong place at the wrong time, pal," Alex said. "I would have let you live, but you fucked my girl. Nobody fucks her but me. So, ya gotta go—right off the fucking cliff. Bye, asshole."

And with that, they tossed Jasper Hunter over the

cliff. He screamed all the way down. His body exploded like a watermelon being dropped when it hit the rocks below. The twins walked back to the mansion and entered through the glass doors that led to the swimming pool. They were about to go upstairs when the doorbell rang.

"Who the fuck is that at this hour?" Alex shouted.

# CHAPTER 12

Keyth was dead to the world, snoring softly in my ear. We had fallen asleep on the bathroom floor after seriously getting our swerve on. With the air conditioner on full blast, the chill in the air awakened me.

"Wake up, honey," I said, and shook my swarthy husband.

"Huh?" He grunted. "What time is it?"

I started to say what difference does it make, but I didn't. I looked at my watch. "It's eleven," I said. "Don't you want to get off the cold floor and get in bed?"

"Yeah, baby. In a couple of minutes," he said and began snoring again.

I laughed a little. I knew he was going to say that. He always does. But over the years, I've learned that it's easier to get him up if I let him sleep a little longer and shake him again. Usually I wait about thirty seconds or so, and then shake him again. I looked at my watch. About a minute had passed.

"Keyth, let's get up, baby," I said a little more forcefully.

"Okay. What time is it?"

"Twelve o' clock," I lied.

"Okay," he said and picked up his two hundred-twenty pounds from the bathroom floor and staggered into the bedroom. He fell on top of the bed and was fast asleep again.

I went to the closet, grabbed a blanket and covered his naked body. I went into the adjoining room to check on my daughter. She was also snoring. I love my husband, my daughter, and our life together. We're very lucky. I thought about my partner, Kelly McPherson, who had had terrible luck with men. She was a beautiful woman and had no problems getting a man, but keeping a man was a different story. Kelly would leave a man at the drop of a hat and have a new suitor that very day. I wondered what she would do when her looks faded. I wanted to remind her that we would arrive in Washington at eight-fifty p.m., so I picked up the phone and called her. I knew she'd be up reading. She had told me she liked doing most of her reading late at night when her children were asleep.

# CHAPTER 13

Kelly McPherson answered the phone. "I know what time the plane lands, Phoenix," she said. "You do know that Washington is three friggin' hours ahead of Los Angeles, right? I mean, you do know that it's two a.m. here, right?"

I laughed. "How'd you know it was me?" I said.

She laughed. "Who the hell else is going to be calling me from the Universal City Hilton?"

"The technology these days," I said sarcastically. "Were you asleep?"

"Hell no. Just sitting here reading an Eric Jerome Dickey book."

"Which one?"

"*Cheaters*. Why? You want to read it when I'm done? Is that why you called this late?"

"Of course. Why else would I call?"

"You want my best guess, Phoenix?"

I could tell she was smiling when she asked the question. "Yeah, Kelly. Your best guess."

"Okay, knowing a hard-core FBI agent like you,

you probably saw the article in *USA Today* about the high-profile murder of a local warden and his wife. I think you were puzzled as hell, probably bothered you all friggin' day. Bothered you so much in fact that you couldn't wait until tomorrow to talk to me about it. How am I doing?"

I smiled. That's how it is when you've been partnered with someone for as long as Kelly and I have been. You know each other so well. You're almost like a set of identical twins.

"Bothered you all day, too, huh, Kelly?"

"Sho' did," she said.

Kelly McPherson is white, but she can speak in the Black English vernacular and sound authentic when it suits her; unlike so many of the morning news anchorwomen, who learn a popular word or phrase and still sound too proper when they say it.

"So who's running the show on this one, Kelly?"

"The locals."

"Are they sharing?"

"Haven't asked, to be honest. I've been on my best behavior, so I'm sure I could find something out."

"Would you?" I asked.

"Sure. I'll look into it tomorrow."

"How's the arm and the leg?" I asked her. Coco Nimburu had broken them during an altercation.

"They're as good as new. Better, if you believe

what they say about a clean break. Did you sprinkle her ashes at the studio?"

"Yeah, I did it."

"Well, I've been working out at your dojo on the wooden dummy like you suggested. That shit is hard on the arms, girl."

"Yeah, but it toughens them up. Keep working at it."

"We're still going to work out together at the dojo though, right, Phoenix?"

"Of course. Anyway, I'm gonna go. See ya tomorrow night."

# CHAPTER 14

Sam looked through the peephole and saw a man with a briefcase standing there with an armed uniformed guard. The man was well dressed, sporting a thin pin-striped suit, a white shirt, a black polka dot tie, and a matching handkerchief. The uniformed guard was at least six feet tall, two hundred pounds of steel wrapped around flesh and bones. His sidearm was a Smith and Wesson .38-caliber revolver.

"Alex," Sam said. "It's a rent-a-cop and a banker."

"Ask him what he wants," Alex said.

Sam hit the intercom button. "Who is it?"

"Charles Kirkwood of Kirkwood Jewelers. I'm here at Jasper Hunter's request. Is he available?"

Sam turned off the intercom. "Alex, hand me the baton," Sam said, and then hit the intercom button again. "Just a second."

Just as Sam opened the door, Heather, who had somehow freed herself, came running down the stairs.

Her hands were still held tightly behind her back with a plastic strap. The tape was still covering her mouth.

Charles Kirkwood's eyes seemed to swell to twice their size when he saw the frightened woman. He was so stunned by the visual that he became temporarily paralyzed and stone-faced.

The uniformed guard had his hand on his Smith and Wesson, on the verge of pulling it out of its holster. Sam zapped him with the baton.

"What the hell is this going on?" Kirkwood asked in a voice that quivered uncontrollably as he spoke.

"Welcome to the party, Charles," Sam said, and zapped him with the baton.

Alex grabbed Heather and stopped her from running out the door. They used the plastic straps to tie up Kirkwood and the guard. Then they strapped Heather's ankles again.

Alex opened Kirkwood's briefcase and found a jewelry case, which contained a 10-karat choker littered with diamonds, and matching stud earrings. According to the enclosed MasterCard receipt signed by Jasper Hunter, the ensemble was worth $100,000.

The twins filled the champagne bucket with ice water, then hoisted their new captives on their shoulders, and carried them out to the bluffs.

# CHAPTER 15

Ice cold water splashed in the faces of Charles Kirkwood and the uniformed guard, waking them out of a forced hibernation. They opened their eyes and realized that they were at the cutting edge of an eight hundred-foot escarpment. Above them, a starry firmament and a full glowing moon.

"How shall we do it, boys?" Alex asked. "One at a time? Or all together?"

Charles Kirkwood was asking why when Sam pushed them both over the side, which caused his words to linger in the air as he plummeted downward and crashed into the waiting rocks.

The twins returned to the mansion and found Heather trying to escape again. Like a snake, she had slithered to the French doors in the foyer, somehow got on her feet, and was attempting to open the door.

Sam grabbed her arm. "Someone has been very naughty. And for that offense, you will be scourged until I grow weary of purging your transgressions against me. But first, I'm going to give you a small taste of what we had to endure to be here on this momentous occasion."

After returning to the master bedroom, the twins closed the vertical blinds. Someone with a telescope could be watching them, and they needed privacy so that they could enjoy the moment they had waited for.

"You wanna hear some music, girls?" Alex asked, walking over to the wall-enclosed Kenwood stereo system to the left of the fireplace. "Let's see. What are our choices? Ah! Here's one I know you're going to enjoy." Alex put in the disc, hit a few buttons on the CD player, and turned the stereo volume up to almost full blast. A few seconds later, Janet Jackson's "Son of a Gun" began playing.

*"Ha! Ha! Hoo! Hoo!...thought you'd get the money too... greedy muthafuckas try to have their cake and eat, too."*

Sam retrieved a pair of seamstress shears from the backpack and cut off Heather's designer clothing. Completely nude, she lay on the bed without moving, neither crying nor attempting to speak. She knew what was about to happen but believed that if she were a willing participant, she could barter for her life after the deed was done.

Sandra Rhodes and Paula Stevens had regained consciousness. Consumed with fear, warm tears mixed with mascara ran down their painted faces. The two women were trying to say something, but their words couldn't be distinguished from their muffled lamentations. They wanted to live, but when they saw the surgical gloves, they realized that they would not survive the night.

The twins peeled off their clothing and folded them neatly. It was an acquired habit formed in prison. They stood before their captives, proud of their manufactured physiques.

With every stitch of clothing discarded, the women could see that their pubic hair had been shaved, which confirmed their impending doom. They knew no DNA evidence would be left. There would be nothing to lead the police to their killers.

Stretching out on the floor, the twins pumped out their customary five-hundred pushups. Beads of sweat began to form on their muscular backs. Their chins touched the floor and they blew out a loud, "One!" Less than two minutes later, they were at fifty. Fifteen minutes after that they said, "Five hundred."

The twins stood up. Their bodies glistened with perspiration, and their massive organs protruded outward. Their breathing had increased, but they were far from sucking wind. Having warmed themselves up, the twins grabbed the seamstress shears and cut away Heather's plastic strapping, but kept her mouth taped shut.

Sam put the diamond choker around Heather's neck, and then forced the matching diamond studs into her ears. "Hope you like the gifts, Heather," Sam said. "You can thank Jasper Hunter when you see him, which won't be too long from now."

Heather was trying to say something. Alex removed the tape. "Any last words?"

"Please don't do this," Heather said in a voice full of horror and dread. "I'll do anything you ask! Anything! I'll be your woman again, Alex. Please... please...please...let us live."

"Sorry, baby. You're ten years too late," Alex said, feeling a little sorry for her. "You gotta go."

"Alex, did you really expect me not to have anyone for ten years—not even Sandra and Paula?"

"YOU DUMB HO!" Alex shouted. "DO YOU REALLY BELIEVE THIS IS ABOUT YOU FUCKING JASPER HUNTER? YOU INSULT US!" With that, Alex re-taped her mouth.

"Do you believe her, Sam?" Alex asked.

"She's got a lot of fucking nerve, Alex," Sam said.

Heather, Sandra, and Paula looked at each other strangely, as if they couldn't believe what they were hearing. Then Heather mumbled something that got the twins' attention. Alex pulled the tape off again.

"When's the last time you took your meds, Alex?" Heather asked desperately.

Alex laughed. "Haven't taken them in over a month. I don't need them anymore."

"Alex," Heather said as calmly as she could. "You need to take your meds. You're..."Alex re-taped her mouth before she had a chance to finish.

"I'M NOT CRAZY!" Alex shouted.

# CHAPTER 16

The sexual excitement that Heather derived from performing cunnilingus on Sandra had stimulated her tremendously and her love canal had been soaked with its own natural lubricants. But her desire for sex had completely evaporated. Now, she was drier than a Death Valley bone. Her vagina had reverted to its natural collapsed balloon state.

Years ago, the idea of having Alex inside her would have been an aphrodisiac that could not be ignored. After all, it was Alex who had deflowered the young California beauty. Now, sex with Alex would be a burden she would bear, but she would take no pleasure in it.

Heather closed her eyes when Alex climbed on top of her. Resignation registered on her face. She just wanted it over and done with. Then she would be in a position to negotiate their freedom. She clenched her teeth hard and tightened her closed eyes when Alex entered her roughly and pounded her recklessly for about ten minutes. Then Sam took her for a ride.

The twins took turns ravaging and sodomizing all the women until they were satisfied that Heather Connelly, Sandra Rhodes, and Paula Stevens had suffered a shadow of what they had suffered over the course of ten years. Now they were ready for phase two: Punishment.

They forced Heather to snort ten lines of cocaine. A line for each nostril would have been enough to give her a buzz, but the twins wanted her higher than a kite. Plus the drug would dull the pain and they could torture her longer. Not only did they want to kill her; they also wanted to humiliate her. They wanted the police and the media to report that the anointed beauty queen had relapsed.

Heather's eyes were half-closed from the cocaine when the twins forced her into a pair of anti-gravity boots that were connected to an apparatus used for doing sit-ups while hanging upside down. Heather had to be first. After all, she had betrayed the plan they concocted when they were just sixteen years old.

Sandra and Paula were mutual beneficiaries of Heather's double-cross. Heather had married into the Connelly family and acquired a fortune, which she shared with Sandra and Paula. All of the women had come from well-to-do families, but the Connelly fortune made it possible for Sandra and Paula to live well enough to attract and marry rich men who assumed they were wealthy also. Sandra and Paula made sure they were impregnated early in their marriages so that if the men wanted out, they could take half of their wealth and get child support, too. In the meantime, the three women continued the sexual liaison that they had begun at Malibu High.

With Heather still naked and securely in the anti-gravity apparatus, the twins spun the equipment so that she hung upside down and locked it into place. Sam pulled a handcrafted Si Davey Tornado bullwhip from the backpack. It was made of red kangaroo hide, which is ten times the strength of cowhide. Mixed with bark dye, the Tornado bullwhip looked like a thin ten-foot red and black snake.

Suddenly, Sam unleashed a flogging that only a seventeenth-century overseer could appreciate. The bullwhip cracked loudly. It sounded like a small caliber gun being fired. Heather's flesh was ripped to the bone with each lash. Blood splattered everywhere. Her muffled groans only served as an incentive to continue the savagery.

The beating went on for over an hour. Finally, mercifully, Heather passed out. Only then did the flagellation end. After they finished with Heather, they put Sandra Rhodes in the apparatus. She fought hard, but they were far stronger. She was beaten into unconsciousness, too. So was Paula Stevens. Satisfied that they had exacted a certain measure of revenge, they went to the garage and grabbed the yellow and black Poulan Pro chain saw from the back seat of the Hummer and dismembered all three women while they were still alive.

# CHAPTER 17

The phone rang in the Connelly mansion at about seven a.m. the following morning, waking the twins who had slept there with the remains of their victims. They had slept so soundly that they couldn't tell if the phone had rung once or twenty times. Opening their eyes, they saw the previous night's carnage, which was brought to bear by the power of their will. A wry smile appeared when they saw body parts that had been thrown against the bloodstained walls.

Alex and Sam pulled the linen from the bed and negotiated the room as if they were walking through a minefield, avoiding the pools of blood. They were hungry and decided to have some breakfast before they wiped the place clean. Their nonstop flight to Washington, D.C. was scheduled to depart at one p.m. Los Angeles International Airport was only forty-five minutes away, giving them plenty of time.

While the linen splashed and twisted in the washer, the twins made pancakes, sausage, eggs, and hash browns. Alex turned on the nine-inch color television that hung over the refrigerator. They wanted to know what, if anything, the police had found out about the murders of Warden Louis Perkins and his wife, Kathy. They, too, had read the article in the previous day's *USA Today*. But either they had missed the story, or CNN hadn't bothered to cover it.

Sam took a sip of coffee and asked, "You think the police found the maid yet?"

Two days ago, the twins had forced their way into Philip and Linda Houston's home on Wildwood Drive. They were a young couple who, luckily for them, had taken a cruise to Alaska.

"Who knows?" Alex asked. "Turn on the morning news. Maybe we can find out something."

Sam pointed the remote control at the television and changed the channel. A local NBC affiliate was giving a report from the house on Wildwood Drive. A young female was standing in front of the home in the darkness with bright lights being shone on her. Evidently, the report had been given the previous night at eleven. According to the reporter, the Houston family returned and discovered the maid with a butcher knife buried in her chest. The reporter went on to say that the Houstons' yellow Hummer had been stolen.

"Guess we gotta get a new ride to the airport, Sam," Alex said.

"Yeah. That's fine. I wanted to drive the Diablo anyway."

Alex tossed the linen in the dryer after they finished eating and washed the dishes. The telephone on the kitchen counter rang loudly. After six rings, the answering machine played a recording. Then the voice of a child could be heard. Alex looked at the caller ID. The call was coming from Sandra Rhodes' home.

"Mrs. Connelly, this is Brett Rhodes Jr. I'm calling to remind my mother that I have a gymnastics class at ten o'clock. I called earlier but no one answered. It's eight o'clock. If she doesn't call by nine, I'll ride my bike down there and wake you guys up. Bye."

"Too bad, kid," Sam began. "Your mother won't be waking up ever again."

"Sam, we gotta get outta here—now!" Alex said. "We can't let her kid find her like that; no matter how we feel about them."

"What do you propose we do, take the kid to gymnastics for her?" Sam asked.

"No, we clean this place up, call 911 on our way out, and get to the airport before the shit hits the fan. We have more people to see. We must stay on schedule; otherwise our plans may be interrupted prematurely."

"Agreed," Sam said. "Let's wipe the kitchen down and go."

The twins dialed 911 and left the phone off the hook. Then they got into the Diablo and headed for LAX.

# CHAPTER 18

The first-class passengers of flight 1131 were being told to board the Boeing 747. The twins walked to the tunneled entrance where the United Airlines attendant checked their tickets. As they stood in line, they thought they saw a familiar figure. Although they were anxious to know if they were right, they could wait. After all, they were all sitting in first-class.

Five minutes later, the first-class passengers were putting their personal belongings in the overhead hatches. The twins watched the figure they thought they recognized as long as they could without drawing attention to themselves. Finally, the figure turned around. It was her. The woman they had seen on television with President Davidson last month while they were still in prison. Although they couldn't remember her name, they knew she was an FBI agent.

As luck would have it, they were sitting right across the aisle from her. She was traveling with a man and a little girl. The twins looked at the diamond ring the woman wore and assumed that the man was her husband and the little girl was her daughter. The woman looked at the twins as if she could feel them staring at her. The twins looked away, then looked at her again. When the woman looked at them again, Alex said, "I do apologize, Miss, but you look so familiar."

The woman smiled. "I get that all the time. People think I resemble Jada Pinkett."

"Who?" Alex frowned.

"You know...the actress."

"I'm sorry. I was thinking of someone else. I'm sure I saw you on television a month or so ago with the president."

"Oh, yeah. I forgot about that. Yes, that was me," she said.

Alex sensed that she was about to introduce herself, which meant they would exchange names. Meeting the FBI agent they had seen on television was so unexpected.

"Don't tell me. It's right on the tip of my tongue. It's a city in the Southwest, I think. Phoenix, isn't it? I remember now. I'm Alex. Pleased to meet you."

Alex didn't want to give her natural curiosity a chance to take over and kept on talking. "Did you hear about that terrible murder in Malibu last night?

A maid was found with a butcher knife in her chest. Saw it on the news this morning."

Sam knew to remain quiet. Alex was far more outgoing and so much better at dealing with strangers.

"Yeah, I saw that this morning also. Terrible thing. Just terrible."

"As an FBI agent, how would you handle that?" Alex continued.

Keyth grunted and Phoenix knew why. They hadn't even taken off yet, and Phoenix was already working on yet another case. Keyth and Phoenix had agreed that she would take an extended vacation after her problems with Coco Nimburu. But Phoenix needed to get back to work. She needed the challenge and the intrigue of the chase. Keyth understood, but he thought that now would be a good time for them to have another baby. Phoenix had told him she would think about it.

"Well, the first thing I'd do is go to the crime scene and look around for things that the killer may have left behind. Fingerprints, blood, footprints, anything out of the ordinary. Then we establish time of death, eliminate the people who couldn't have done it and focus the search on those who could have. In these cases, it's usually someone the victim knew. If the victim is a husband, we check out the wife and vice versa. If they check out, we expand our search."

The 747 taxied to the end of the runway and prepared for take-off. A few minutes later the plane picked up speed down the bumpy runway and they were in the air.

Alex noticed that Phoenix had a bit of an ego and was trying to figure out the best way to use it against her; just in case they tangled in the future. But for now, Alex needed to keep her talking about herself, or the FBI. Otherwise, she would start asking questions. And if that happened, Phoenix may learn something, seemingly insignificant, that could lead to their capture later.

"So did you catch the judge's killer that way?" Alex asked.

"No. That was a special case, but I caught her," Phoenix couldn't help saying.

That settled it for Alex. Phoenix was an egomaniac and if it came down to it, that weakness would be used against her. Alex was smiling and didn't realize it.

"What?" Phoenix asked, confused as to why Alex was smiling.

"Oh, nothing. I was just thinking that Americans are lucky to have dedicated agents like you watching over us while we sleep."

The 747 leveled off and the flight attendant had begun to serve beverages. The lights dimmed. A movie was about to start. Alex ordered a chardonnay, and then asked what movie they were going to watch.

"*Crouching Tiger, Hidden Dragon*," the attendant said.

"What's that about?" Alex asked the attendant. "Is that a cartoon?"

"No," Phoenix interrupted. "It's an Oscar-winning martial arts film."

"Really? A martial arts film won an Oscar, huh?" Alex said. "Last time I watched the Oscars was about ten years ago. If memory serves, *Unforgiven* won the Oscar for picture of the year. I guess if a Western can win, a martial arts picture can win, too."

"Do you have something against martial arts films?" Phoenix said straight-faced.

"Something tells me you're a huge fan of martial arts films, huh?"

"That and more. I'm a Grandmaster of Shaolin Kung Fu," Phoenix said proudly. "I trained for twelve years with Master Ying Ming Lo. I was six years old when I started."

"I see." Alex smiled. "So I guess you can break a pile of bricks with your forehead, huh?"

Suddenly serious, Phoenix said, "Kung Fu is more than breaking bricks and boards. It's a way of life— a philosophy, if you will."

"I suppose you teach the art, too."

"As a matter of fact, I do."

"And that's how you caught the judge's killer?"

"In a manner of speaking, yes. The judge's killer was a martial artist also. One of the best in the world."

"I see, so that makes you one of the best in the world, doesn't it?"

"Well, yes."

The movie was starting. Alex put on the earphones and said, "I'll have to make sure I watch the movie closely so I learn what you're capable of."

Phoenix smiled.

Alex studied the movements of Zhang Zhi and Michelle Yeoh and was impressed with their balance and flexibility.

Alex whispered, "Can you do that?"

"Yes."

"How do I contact you if I ever want to take lessons?"

Phoenix handed Alex her FBI business card. Alex smiled and continued studying the film.

# CHAPTER 19

K elly McPherson and I met in the food court at Union Station for lunch at about noon. Kelly had beef fried rice and sweet and sour chicken. I had a salad and tea. As we ate, Kelly filled me in on the Perkins murders.

"The locals don't give a damn about the murders, Phoenix," Kelly told me. "They're looking into the murders, but they believe the warden got what he deserved."

"What about the wife? Do they think she deserved it, too?" I asked rhetorically.

Kelly curled her lips and rolled her eyes, then continued, "The warden was in cahoots with a local drug dealer named Nelson Blake. Nelson was supplying the gangs with heroin and cocaine. One of the guards at the prison made a deal for giving up Nelson and the other guards."

"So have they picked up the suspect?"

"Not yet," Kelly said, looking over my shoulder. "Guess who made acting director?"

I turned around. Kortney Malone was coming toward our table. Kortney and I had been at Quantico together ten years ago. She was a Southern belle from Nashville, Tennessee. Kortney made a name for herself in the Office of Professional Responsibility. She had played an instrumental role in having over fifty agents fired for offenses ranging from stealing drugs from the evidence room to falsifying official FBI documents.

The Joann Ellard and Mia Roscoe case immediately came to mind. They had met a couple of guys on the internet who were members of a D.C. swingers club. Both agents had been shot during a robbery at the club. When asked why they were there, they said friends had invited them and it was their first visit. But when Kortney questioned the bartender and other guests, they all knew the agents as regulars.

Director St. Clair was willing to sweep the lying under the rug, but Kortney wouldn't let it go. She was like a dog on a bone. Kortney argued that an agent should have never been in a position like that. If the guests found out they were FBI agents, they could have been blackmailed into giving up government secrets. Eventually, St. Clair relented and they were both fired.

"Hi, ladies," Kortney said with a Tennessee accent. "Mind if I join you?"

"Well, uh," Kelly stammered.

# CHAPTER 20

**K**ortney Malone sat down as if she didn't hear Kelly's hesitant objection. She was a good-looking black woman, very well-dressed, sporting a gold skirt suit with thick navy stripes and matching two-toned pumps. She had toned thighs and calves, medium-sized breasts and a large behind. Seeing her reminded me of Sir Mixalot's rap recording "Baby Got Back." Kortney was having jumbo shrimp with fries and a kiwi strawberry Snapple.

"Damn shame about Assistant Director Michelson, huh, Kortney?" Kelly jabbed.

Lawrence Michelson and Kortney Malone had been lovers a few years back. Michelson would go to the academy under the guise of looking over the graduating classes, but he was actually there to check out the women. If he saw a woman he wanted, he made sure she was assigned to the D.C. area.

"Yeah, it was. Hard to tell the criminals from the cops, huh. Kelly?" Kortney retorted, and sprayed some ketchup on her fries.

Kelly's bottom lip quivered. She stopped eating and stared at Kortney, like she wanted to jab her in the throat with her fork. I was thinking there was no way this could turn out good for Kelly if the verbal sparring continued. Kortney was the acting FBI director with a reputation for suspending and firing agents. Kelly was a liaison agent assigned to D.C. Metro, a position she loved. Kortney could have her reassigned to Alaska.

"Sooooo, Kortney, how do you like being the acting boss?" I asked to remind Kelly of who she was being smart with. I knew she realized it, but sometimes Kelly didn't know when to shut up.

"What's that supposed to mean?" Kortney asked flippantly. "Nobody gave me the position. There's been too much bullshit going on in the bureau under St. Clair. President Davidson wants me to clean up his mess. Which reminds me, Agent Perry, I read your report on the Nimburu killing. When your extended vacation is over, I have some questions for you."

"Kortney," I said, "don't you think you're being a little paranoid?"

"Paranoia is a reasonable strategy given the current state of the bureau, wouldn't you say?"

That settled it for me. I wasn't going back to work for another month. Kortney was on a witch-hunt and I wasn't going to be part of it—at least not for a while anyway. I was very disappointed because I was ready to return to duty. But I wasn't about to be grilled about a case that I had already put to bed.

"Look, Kortney," I said. "I admire and respect what you've done in the OPR. But you have to be careful that you don't root out the wheat with the tare."

"I think it's a mistake to have agents snitching on each other," Kelly interjected.

"And I think it's a mistake for law enforcement officers to adapt the language of criminals, Agent McPherson."

Kelly frowned. She had no idea what Kortney was talking about. But I did. I knew exactly what she was talking about.

"You call it snitching, Agent McPherson. I, however, call it applying the law equally across the board. Especially when cops are involved. If we're not careful, the FBI will be reduced to the same despicable status as the New York and Los Angeles police departments. Is that what you want? Do you want to be thought of as a bureau that the people can't trust? That's not why I became an FBI agent. If I have to fire a hundred agents to regain our collective fidelity, our collective bravery, and our collective integrity, that's what I'm going to do. I need seasoned agents with enough intestinal fortitude to stay the course, to point out the bad agents so that we can preserve the dignity and the purity of the oath we took. And if you think that's snitching, you don't belong in the bureau." Kortney looked at me, and continued. "If the wheat, which outnumber the tare, would stand and be counted, the tare wouldn't chock out the wheat."

"Fine, Kortney," I said. "I'm all for cleaning up the bureau, but again, be careful. That's all I'm saying."

Kelly's cell chimed a musical tune that sounded like "Rhapsody in Blue." She flipped open the phone and answered the call. It was police headquarters, she told me. Apparently, Nelson Blake had turned himself in.

# CHAPTER 21

D etective Aaron McDonald was one of the toughest cops in the nation's capital. At six four and two hundred-fifty pounds with coal black skin, even at forty-two, he looked as if he could play linebacker for the Washington Redskins. He was a twenty-year veteran who had put away more than his share of slime. He worked the hard-core D.C. ghettos and was a friend to the innocent people who lived there. McDonald had learned that Warden Perkins was involved with Nelson Blake from a street dealer named Bony Davis. That bit of information led McDonald to the prison where he persuaded a guard to tell all that he knew.

McDonald was well into the interrogation of Nelson Blake by the time we got to headquarters. He had tangled with Blake numerous times on trafficking charges, but the district attorney's office was unable to convict him. Blake was smart and had the right connections to stay one step ahead of the police.

It always angered McDonald when intelligent black men decided to take the quick path to riches rather than use their intelligence to help turn the black community around. Men like Nelson Blake made his job more difficult because the children in D.C. ghettos tended to look up to the Nelson Blakes of the world and make the same choices. But this time, it would be different. This time they had a witness who had signed a confession and had named Nelson Blake as the prison's supplier.

We were standing behind the two-way mirror listening to the interview. Blake maintained a cool exterior as he listened to Detective McDonald, like he wasn't the least bit worried. He was very dapper in his manner of dress, wearing a black silk collarless suit and black Armani shoes. He was almost arrogant, but not quite.

"Where were you last Saturday night?" Detective McDonald asked.

Blake just stared at the detective. He seemed to be thinking, calculating.

"Look, help yourself out. We know you were the one supplying the warden with drugs. What happened between you? Was he stealing from you? How was his wife involved?"

Blake looked at the two-way mirror.

"You're looking at a double murder; special circumstances. You and your crew raped and murdered the warden's wife. The DA's office's hands are tied. You're gonna fry for this, son. They'll say your business with him had nothing to do with his wife. They'll put her picture up so the jury can see what she looked like before you cut her up with that bullwhip. Then the DA will tell the jury about her being a Big Sister volunteer, and being a Red Cross volunteer, and how everyone loved her.

"Then, you know what the DA will do, don't you? Yeah, you know. They'll put up the autopsy photos. They're going to show her back all cut up, her black and blue wrists from being tied so tightly that her circulation was cut off. Then come the photographs of her vagina that had been ripped up from repeated rape. They couldn't get O.J. But they'll get a drug-dealing nigga like you. They'll come back with a conviction in ten minutes. Don't throw your life away, son. Confess and make it easy on yourself."

Blake looked at his diamond-studded Rolex like he had all the time in the world and said, "I want an attorney. Can I make my phone call now?"

Detective McDonald was about to say something more when Blake put up his hand and said, "Untuh, detective. The second I ask for a lawyer, all questioning stops. And by the way, the District of Columbia doesn't have the death penalty. I'm surprised a seasoned veteran like you would try some shit like that. Now, be a good little boy and get me a phone."

McDonald mumbled something before leaving the room. Blake looked at the two-way mirror and winked. Kelly and I stared at him. He knew what I knew. The police didn't have anything on him. No drug dealer would leave the money and the drugs. McDonald was convinced that Blake knew something, and had gambled that he could get Blake to give up information to save his own skin. It didn't work. Back to square one. If Blake didn't do it, who did? And if money wasn't a motive, what was? I wondered.

Detective McDonald came back into the interview room with a phone. He plugged it in. Blake picked up the receiver and hit the buttons on the phone quickly, as if he'd made the call every day of his life.

"Yeah, Jimmy," Blake said, still looking at the two-way mirror. "Nelson Blake here. Is the boss in?" A few seconds later, Nelson was speaking again. "Yeah, man, this is Blake. I'm in a jam. Can you talk to your brother for me, man? Easiest money he'll ever make." He looked at Detective McDonald. "The nation's capital is full of stupid cops. They think a lowlife like me would kill a prison warden, rape his white wife, and leave the goddamn money and drugs."

Blake laughed loudly. I could only assume that whomever he was talking to was laughing as well.

"Yeah, man," Blake continued. "I guess these muthafuckas gotta justify their salaries somehow." He laughed again. "So, brotha, you think you can get him to take my case, or what? So, he's already in D.C.? Call his cell, man. I wanna be outta this muthafucka by six." He looked at his Rolex. "It's one-thirty now." Blake was quiet again. "Uh-huh, yeah man. It's bullshit. They don't know who did it, so these dumb bastards come after my ass."

A few seconds later, Blake hung up the phone and smiled at Detective McDonald who was seething.

"Don't even think about it, man," Blake said in a cool street tone. "If you touch me, here's what's going to happen. First, I'ma end up kickin' yo' ass, then I'll sue you for that cheap-ass house you live in."

McDonald flung the table out of the way and had Blake, who was laughing hysterically, up against the wall. Kelly and I raced into the room.

"Somebody better talk to this man." Blake laughed. "He 'bout tuh fuck around and lose his pension."

# CHAPTER 22

Sterling Wise was already in the D.C. area, attempting to work out football contracts for a couple of players for the Redskins. Kelly and I were surprised to see him. When I asked him how he knew the defendant, he told me that his older brother, Jericho, had called him from the Caymans and asked him to defend Nelson Blake.

Kelly and I were sitting in the last row of the courtroom on red-cushioned seats, watching Sterling argue for the release of Nelson Blake before Judge Bauer. Sterling was tall, dark, in the black sense of the word, and handsome. He wore an expensive, light- colored suit with a paisley tie.

"Your Honor," Sterling was saying. "These charges are ludicrous. The DA doesn't have any evidence whatsoever. No fingerprints, no traces of DNA, no threats, nothing. All they have is the word of a guard who was involved with the trafficking himself. But more importantly, Your Honor, the DA claims that my client is a notorious drug dealer. Yet, this same so-called drug dealer left several kilos of cocaine, and over forty thousand dollars in plain sight. Furthermore, the victims were beaten with a bullwhip and dismembered with a chain saw. The police searched my client's home and car and found nothing. No whip, no chain saw, not even carpet fibers from the victims' home. Finally, Your Honor, when my client learned that he was wanted for questioning, he came to the police; they didn't have to hunt him down. All of this is consistent with an innocent man. These charges should be dropped and Nelson Blake should be released immediately."

"Mr. Vanzant?" Judge Bauer said to the District Attorney.

"Your Honor, Mr. Blake has been identified as the man who supplied the prison with the drugs. We believe he knows who committed the crime and should be held in custody for further questioning."

"Hearsay, Your Honor," Sterling interjected. "The prison guard has never even seen the defendant. He's going by what he heard, not what he knows."

"Mr. Vanzant, if that's all you have..." Judge Bauer said.

"Your Honor, I respectfully request that you allow us to hold him for further questioning," Vanzant said. "We believe we can get corroboration from the other guards, but as of now, no one is talking."

"Then my hands are tied, counsel," Judge Bauer said and slammed the mallet on the gavel. "You're free to go, Mr. Blake."

I had told Sterling that I thought the charges were a sham and that they shouldn't have even arrested his client. I also reminded him that I had saved his life a month or so ago in Denver. He promised to speak to Blake on my behalf but stopped short of promising an interview, which is exactly what I wanted. Nelson Blake was a notorious drug dealer and probably a murderer, too, but he didn't have anything to do with the Perkins' murders. However, that didn't mean he didn't know who had committed the murders.

# CHAPTER 23

Jerry and Terry followed Sarah Lawford to her home at 1619 East Continental Boulevard in Arlington, Virginia. The two-story colonial was well-kept and neat, with assorted plants on either side of the stairs that led to the porch. The house was powder blue and white with old-fashioned wood shutters. The place looked as if it had been built specifically for a perfect little family with a perfect little wife and hubby team and perfect little crumbsnatchers. But Sarah Lawford wasn't married and she didn't have any children. She lived alone.

Sarah Lawford parked her black Volkswagen Jetta in front of the white picket fence that enclosed her home and popped the trunk. She got out and walked to the rear of the car. Sarah was just barely five feet tall with heels on, but she was well put together and prettier than ninety percent of the actresses in Hollywood. She was so good-looking that most men didn't bother asking her out, believing that such a gorgeous woman already had to have a man eating out her hands. But nothing was further from the truth. She had spent many lonely nights in the house on Continental Boulevard.

Part of the reason she was alone on most nights was because she was a schoolteacher at Matthew Henson Academy. With the exception of two weeks for Christmas vacation, two weeks for spring break, two weeks before the start of the summer session, and another two weeks before the start of the fall session, Henson students went to school six days a week forty-four weeks a year. With a demanding schedule like that, Sarah barely had time for herself, let alone a significant other. However, when Bernard Rodgers, who taught trigonometry, joined the faculty during the spring session, Sarah Lawford made sure he knew she was down-to-earth and available. A whirlwind romance developed and they were going to marry and honeymoon before the start of the fall session in Las Vegas at the Mandalay Bay Hotel.

Sarah grabbed two bags of groceries and started walking toward the white picket fence. She saw one of her students, a bright-eyed boy named Luther Pleasant, who happened to be rollerblading in her direction.

Luther was black, just eight years old and a mathematical wizard with a schoolboy crush on Miss Lawford. He skated around Sarah in a circle with ease, smiling as he showed off his incredible balance.

"Hi, Mr. Pleasant," Sarah said. Calling students by their surname was a part of the school's charter. When Anthony George, the presiding principal, founded the school ten years earlier, he believed that children needed to be taught to respect themselves as well as others. One way to do that, he believed, was by having the teachers call the boys Mister and the girls Miss along with their surnames. The children were not allowed to use first names either.

"Hi, Miss Lawford!" Luther beamed.

"Will you help me take my groceries into the house?" Sarah asked the youngster.

"Sure, Miss Lawford." Luther smiled.

"Just grab one bag at a time, okay?" Sarah said, sensing that the boy would try to impress her and drop everything all over the ground. "And make sure you take off your rollerblades before you come into the house."

"Okay, Miss Lawford," Luther said.

After they finished taking in the bags, Sarah offered Luther five dollars for services rendered, but he refused. Sarah then promised to let him help her make some peanut butter cookies for the class later that week and he agreed. After Luther left,

Sarah turned on her stereo system and hit a couple of buttons on the CD player. A few seconds later "Brothers Hang On," a tune on MC Hammer's "Too Legit To Quit" CD began. Sarah sang along.

*"My mind is poisoned from the picture that I see... The hookers or the killers always seem to look at me... BLACK"*

Ding-dong! The doorbell chimed over the music. Sarah went to the door and looked through the peephole. There were two men standing on her porch wearing Capitol City Cable overalls. The Arlington area was scheduled to receive the new digital cable so she opened the door. The men were twins with short crewcut hairstyles. Zap! Terry touched her with a stun baton.

# CHAPTER 24

The last thing Sarah Lawford remembered was opening her front door and being zapped by a black baton. She opened her eyes and realized that she was nude, gagged, and tied to her own bed with her legs spread eagle. Disoriented, she began to panic. To her knowledge, she hadn't done anything wrong.

Sarah had taught at Matthew Henson School for seven years. She got along famously with the other members of the faculty and all of her students liked her. She had the unique ability to make all her students feel as if they were her favorite pupils.

As Sarah struggled fruitlessly to free herself, she could hear someone moving around; someone was still in her room. She recognized the two men from Capitol City Cable. They were saying something to each other, but she couldn't understand what they were saying. One of them looked back at her and smiled. He picked up something off the floor and was walking over to the bed. As he got closer, Sarah could tell that the man had a leather whip in his hand.

He sat down on the bed and looked down into Sarah's brown eyes. The terror he saw in them excited him. The man rubbed the whip all over her body, and in small circles around her stiff nipples. The other man was busy putting something together. Suddenly, the man with the whip started to disrobe. That's when Sarah's eyes began to bulge out of her head. She knew that the two men intended to rape her. She struggled to free herself, but it was no use. Sarah Lawford was going to be a statistic.

Before she knew it, the man who had had the whip was pushing himself inside her. Sarah whimpered like a wounded animal as the intruder brutalized her for what seemed like an eternity. Unrelenting tears fell from the corners of her eyes, but the intruder was merciless. After thirty minutes of ruthless savagery, the man got off her and the other man got on top of her and continued where his twin left off.

When they finished ravaging her, they strapped her into the portable gravity boots upside down. With whips in hand, the beating began. The whip crackled loudly and Sarah's delicate body convulsed. Her muffled cries and groans were so terrible that only the Marquis de Sade could have listened to the flogging without covering his ears. One stinging blow after another, almost in synchronized rhythm, ripped away flesh all the way down to the bone. The lashing continued until unconsciousness ripped Sarah Lawford away from the brutality that seemed to go on forever. Then they dismembered her.

# CHAPTER 25

Nelson Blake decided to get out of town while the getting was good, he told Sterling. He had decided to take a vacation in the Caymans where Jericho Wise owned the Renegade Hotel and Casino. He feared the police might get creative and plant some evidence so that they could arrest him again. I knew if I was going to find out anything about what really happened to the warden and his wife, I would have to get it from him before he left the country. There was an eight-thirty flight leaving Dulles for the Caymans and Nelson Blake said he would definitely be on it.

We all rode in Sterling's limousine to the airport. But I wanted to speak to Blake alone. I thought that was the best way to get some vital information out of him. Blake and I sat at a table at T.G.I. Friday's not far from gate D19. Sterling and Kelly sat a few tables from us.

Blake stared at me while I questioned him. I could tell that he wanted me. In another place, in another time, if I weren't married, and if he wasn't a criminal, I might go for the young man. There was something attractive about him. Perhaps it was his cool exterior. Or maybe it was the danger that seemed to seep from his pores. Whatever it was, it was alluring, but I remained professional.

"Listen, Blake," I began. "I know you weren't involved with the Perkins murders. The drug dealing is another matter altogether. We may not be able to prove that you were supplying the prison, but I know you were." I bluffed. "However, I'm not interested in that crime. I'm interested in the murders. What can you tell me about them?"

Blake smiled broadly. "You know, girl, you sho' is sexy."

"Thank you," I said, then went right back to work on him. "Did the warden have enemies inside the prison? Maybe one of the guards wasn't getting enough of the cut?"

"I guess that ring means you married, huh?" Blake asked.

I didn't want to turn him against me, so I figured I'd better play along for a while. I had about two hours before his plane took off. If I became argumentative, he may not tell me anything at all.

"Yes," I said and showed him the ring up close.

"Humpf," he grunted. "If I had you, I'da bought you one them Zsa Zsa Gabor rings. You know, one that would light up the night when the moonlight hit that bad boy. Like Alicia Keys said, 'Baby, you know you worth it.'"

I smiled. "I'm married, Nelson. I have an eight-year-old daughter, too. Please don't interfere with that."

"So you happy?" he asked.

I kind of laughed a little. Shook my head. "You know, Nelson, it always amazes me when people ask that question. It's like if you say I'm unhappy, then somehow you're no longer married or something. But, to answer your question, I'm very happy. Okay? Now, will you answer some of my questions before your plane takes off?"

"Yeah, okay. What do you wanna know?"

"What are your thoughts on the warden's murder? If you had to guess, who would you say did it? Who would have that big of a grudge to bullwhip them like they were runaway slaves?"

"I have no idea. None whatsoever. Wasn't no dealer though. If I had to guess, I'd look at the recently paroled inmates. Perkins was no choirboy. Allowed the prisoners to do pretty much what they wanted as long as nobody got killed. See, killin' would bring too much unwanted heat. There would be an external investigation. Perkins couldn't control that. So as long as nobody got killed, we all made money. Serious money. The warden, me, the guards and the gangs. And the prisoners got all the drugs they wanted."

"So who would be pissed if everybody was getting what they wanted?"

"The hell if I know. If I did, I'd waste whoever it was myself. Deals like that don't get no sweeter. On the other hand, Perkins let a lot of sexual abuse go on. Prostitution rings, gang bangin' other prisoners—all kinds of shit went on in that prison. You had to be a gang member or a Muslim to avoid being turned out."

# CHAPTER 26

"There's something different about you, Sterling," Kelly began. "What is it?"

"What do you mean?" Sterling asked, but he knew exactly what she was talking about.

Sterling had been a lady's man all of his life. But with the murder of his assistant, he had begun to reflect on his playboy lifestyle. In the last month he had thought about Vanessa Wright, his former live-in girlfriend, and decided to try and get her back.

"You just seem different," Kelly repeated. She didn't see the same lust in his eyes that she'd seen in the Denver airport when they met. A month ago, Kelly believed that Sterling found her attractive. Were it not for the tragedy that befell them, he probably would have made a move on her. "How have you been getting along since your assistant died? Tiffany was her name, wasn't it?"

"Yes, her name was Tiffany," Sterling acknowledged. "She had been with me for about ten years.

She was just eighteen years old when I met her. She was a student at the University of San Francisco and working part-time for the District Attorney's office. But to answer your question, I've been better."

"So you used to prosecute criminals, huh?" Kelly smiled.

"Yeah, for about seven years. Never lost a case." He grinned proudly.

"What made you leave the DA's office?"

"I got an offer I couldn't refuse from the most prestigious firm in San Francisco. Ever heard of Daniels, Burgess and Franklin?"

"No. I can't say I have."

"Well, Zachary Daniels is the senior partner and he recruited me after I cleaned their clocks on a murder case." Sterling grinned again.

"It's hard to lose someone you cared about, huh?" Kelly asked.

"Yes."

"Believe me, I know. I've been through the ringer, too," Kelly said. "So Phoenix says you're in town working on contracts for some of the football players."

"Yes. That's correct."

"Do you like being an agent better than you liked being a defense attorney?"

"In some ways. In others no. In a way, athletes are

like criminals in that they are used to having what they want when they want it. I guess that's why so many of them end up in the system after their playing careers are over."

"So what do you do for fun, Sterling?"

"These days I haven't had much fun. The regular season opens in a few weeks and I still have some owners that are playing hardball with some of the veteran players. On the other hand, some of the veterans see what the rookies are making fresh outta college and they're jealous, which I can understand. When you've given your heart and soul to a team and some rookie who hasn't proven his worth comes to camp with a $12 million signing bonus, it gets under their skin. The trick is to find a happy medium—a contract that both parties can live with."

"Well, how much longer are you going to be in town?" Kelly asked.

"A few more days. Why?"

"I was thinking I haven't had much fun myself since Coco Nimburu blew into town and shook up everybody's world. And if you want some company, I thought we could have some coffee or something. Talk, or shoot a game of pool, whatever."

Sterling felt himself stiffen. It was a natural reflex for him. Women came onto him all the time. This was nothing new, but it was different. He found

Kelly attractive, just as any man would. But now he wanted to change his ways. He wanted to stop the bed-hopping and finally go after Vanessa Wright. Nevertheless, he hadn't had sex since he left Denver, almost forty days ago. And his body was telling him he could go after Vanessa later. Right now, it needed to be submerged into some friendly flesh.

"I'll tell you what. I may have some time later this evening and I may not. Sometimes contract talks go late into the night."

"Yeah, sometimes investigations do, too," Kelly said. "Let's just play it by ear."

"Cool," Sterling said.

# CHAPTER 27

Nelson Blake had told me all that I needed to know as far as who the suspects were. He had eliminated himself and anyone from his drug-infested world when he told me that they were all making money. Rarely does a drug dealer have a better set-up. They even had a processing lab inside the prison. There was absolutely no reason to disrupt the free flow of drugs from Norrell. When the warden was killed, everybody lost money and the lab was shut down.

Somehow, the word "money" kept coming up, yet the money wasn't taken. This led me to believe that either the killer didn't need the money, or this was a righteous killing. The killer wanted to expose the warden. Maybe that was the reason for the bullwhip. Maybe the killer wanted to punish Perkins for his crimes. But why the wife? Why scourge her? Why rape? Did she have anything to do with drug dealing? I was baffled.

"Kelly," I said as we zoomed down the Beltway to Arlington in her black Stingray. "What do you think is going on?"

"The hell if I know, Phoenix. I've been thinkin' about the handsome lawyer we just left."

I looked at her. Kelly was smiling from ear-to-ear. I knew what that meant. She was going to screw Sterling. She had already made up her mind.

"Kelly, don't you think..."

She cut me off. "Phoenix, don't. Okay? I know what you're going to say and I don't need to hear it right now. You know what I've been through with Simon, and you know he lost Tiffany. Maybe we need each other right now to move on. You know what they say, 'Nothin' gets you over the last one like the next one.'"

"So Sterling was havin' a thing with Tiffany?" I asked.

"Probably. I mean, she was his personal assistant. All the traveling together. Let's not forget that she was good-looking and so is he. I'd say they were knocking boots."

It was hard for me to understand Kelly's attitude about sex. There had been a lot of traffic between her thighs in the ten years I'd known her. Well, maybe five or six guys aren't a lot these days. I was a virgin when I married Keyth. Call me old-fashioned, call me self-righteous, but I think sex ought to mean more than a romp and a sincere "see ya when I see ya" attitude. But Kelly is my girl, my very best female friend. And if she didn't want to hear it, I wouldn't say it.

"You just make sure you use protection, hear?" I said like I was her mother.

"Yes, Mommy," Kelly said, mimicking Savannah. We laughed.

"We need to get out to Norrell Prison first thing in the morning," I said. "Question some people. Stir things up a bit."

"Sounds good to me," Kelly said. "All those incarcerated men, harder than the cement walls that surround them. This may be just what I need."

We laughed.

I said, "We start with Salaam Khan."

# CHAPTER 28

Sirens blared! Red and blue lights bounced off the homes in my neighborhood. An EMS truck was parked across the street from my house on Continental Boulevard, right in front of Sarah Lawford's house. There were also a couple of police cars and a few media vehicles. I shuddered when I saw the coroner's van. I hoped that it wasn't Sarah. She was one of Savannah's teachers at the Academy. Kelly parked the Stingray. We got out, donned our FBI windbreakers, and flashed our credentials.

As we approached the house, something inside of me prodded me to turn around. I did. I saw Savannah and Jill Fisher, our babysitter, standing on our lawn watching.

"Kelly, I'll be back. My daughter's watching."

Kelly turned around. "Okay, Phoenix. I'll take a look around. See what happened here."

I walked across the street. The closer I got to my daughter, the more evident her grief became. Dry tear stains and a blank stare defined her. I didn't know if she was in shock or what. But I did know that she had seen enough, even though she hadn't seen anything at all. At least, that was my hope.

"Ms. Lawford's dead, isn't she, Mommy?" Savannah managed to say, fighting back the tears that welled up again.

"I don't know, honey," I said. It breaks my heart to see my daughter hurt this way. I hugged her and took her back inside without answering her question. Somebody was dead. That was certain. And in all probability, it was Sarah Lawford. It was her house. I didn't see her outside. Unless she wasn't home, I could only assume it was her that the coroner's office was here to pick up. "Savannah, I think you oughta get some sleep, honey. I'll let you know what happened, if anything, in the morning, okay?"

Without a word, Savannah turned around, walked down the hallway and entered the bathroom. A few seconds later, I heard the water splashing in the bathtub.

"What time did Keyth say he would be home?" I asked Jill.

"He said he would be late."

I looked at my watch. It was nearly ten p.m.

"Make sure Savannah goes to bed when she gets outta the bathtub."

# CHAPTER 29

The crowd that surrounded Sarah Lawford's home had increased substantially since I went inside to talk to my daughter. Looks of concern were on the faces of men and women, blacks and whites alike in our integrated neighborhood.

Initially, Henson Academy was predominantly black. When it was learned that Henson was rated the best in the District of Columbia because of the high academic standards, well-to-do whites and other minority groups began to send their children there in droves. Booster money poured in. Soon the school had state-of-the-art computers, a brand-new gymnasium; an Olympic-sized swimming pool and a fencing team.

Our community was probably the only one in America where whites were moving in, not out. Property values were growing, not declining. More important, our community was rising above the petty differences that plagued the country, becoming a racial cross-section of America. Nevertheless, murder had a way of bringing out the worst in people. Often, people associated a person's deeds with their color and either excused what's happened, or they're shocked by who actually committed the crime.

"What's happened to Miss Lawford, Mrs. Perry?" I heard Luther Pleasant ask me.

I looked down at the boy genius who had asked me a thousand times if he had asked me once to teach him the ancient martial art that had become a major ingredient of who I am.

"I don't know, Luther," I told him. "I haven't been in the house yet."

I opened the white picket fence and walked up the stairs two at a time. Kelly met me at the door. She told me that Detective McDonald was in charge. We knew him and that meant we wouldn't have to throw our weight around. I hated doing it and the cops hated it, too.

I could tell by the look on Kelly's face that whatever happened to Sarah Lawford wasn't good. Kelly and I had worked lots of murder scenes. After a while, we even ate lunch or dinner immediately after leaving a scene. Never have I seen Kelly look so ghastly, so completely appalled.

"What?" I said, unsure if I wanted to know what she had seen.

"The son-of-a-bitch struck again," Kelly told me.

"Who?" I said, unable to distinguish whom she was talking about.

"The same man that killed the warden, killed this woman."

"What?" I heard myself asking in a stupefied daze.

I walked up the stairs, still confused, still flabbergasted at what Kelly had said. D.C. Homicide was on the scene. The mechanized sound of pictures being photographed rang in my dulled senses. A litany of voices buzzed in my ears. Almost in slow motion, I walked into the room, completely unnoticed by D.C. Homicide. Thick puddles of blood were everywhere. Some of it was sprinkled on the wall like it had been squirted. I looked down and I saw Sarah Lawford's head, which had been separated from her body. Her brown eyes seemed to stare at me in unimaginable horror. I knew then that she was alive when this animal, this demon from the bowels of hell, had sliced into her flesh like he was opening a can of soup.

I closed my eyes and shook my head. I remembered the wedding invitation Keyth and I had gotten when we returned from our westward excursion. I could literally see the invitation in my mind, see the wedding bells, smell the newness of the lavender paper the words were printed on. I fought back my tears. I knew this woman. I knew Sarah Lawford. I had been in this home many times. I also knew Bernard Rodgers, her fiancé. This would kill him.

There's nothing more sobering than death, I thought. Nothing penetrates the heart like death. The stench of it. The pain it causes those it leaves in its wake is often unbearable. It awakens you. It shakes you, and makes you realize what's truly important. Death trivializes everything except life itself, ironically its only opposite.

The coroner had turned over Sarah Lawford's torso and was examining the lacerations on her back. I cringed when I saw flesh pulled away from bone. *Oh, my God!* The fact that she actually lived through the flogging was a miracle, I thought. I had seen enough.

# CHAPTER 30

Melted ice cream was dripping on the kitchen floor where it apparently had sat all day on the blue marble table inside one of the grocery bags. Some of the bags were still on the counter, others on the floor. My partner was trying to determine what had happened, I assumed, when I found her in the kitchen.

"Someone came in when she got home, Phoenix," Kelly said. "That explains the melted ice cream."

"So you think she let him in? Which means it was someone she knew," I said. "I don't like where this is going. We know that the bastard who did this is somehow connected to the Perkins murders. Am I to conclude that Sarah Lawford, my daughter's schoolteacher, was somehow involved with Perkins and drugs?"

"That's how it looks, Phoenix," Kelly said sadly. "I know you knew the woman, but hell, think of what we went through last month with Lawrence Michelson. You never know what people are doing. And what about Simon? Who knew what he was up to?"

Kelly had a point but I just didn't see Sarah Lawford, arguably the best teacher, and most liked by all who knew her at the Academy, involved in this sordid business at Norrell Prison. It just didn't make sense. Yet, the evidence would seem to indicate that the same man had murdered three people. Maybe I didn't want to believe it.

"I don't believe it, Kelly," I said firmly. "I don't care what the evidence says. I knew this woman. No way she'd be involved with drugs."

"And that, my friend, is why they don't allow us to handle cases we're too close to. We tend to ignore what's in plain view in a futile attempt to exonerate friends and relatives."

I heard a disturbance coming from outside. It sounded like Bernard Rodgers.

"SARAH!" the man shouted. "Let-me-go! Let-me-go! SARAH! SARAH!"

Next, I heard the clump, clump of someone running up the stairs onto the porch. I knew it was Bernard. I immediately went through the kitchen door and out into the hallway that led to the front door. I saw Bernard Rodgers, all six feet two inches of him. He was well-muscled in his chest and arms. Bernard knew of my martial arts skills but he didn't seem to care. He was determined to get past me and see what had happened to his beloved. I, on the other hand, was determined to stop him. He didn't need to see what that animal had done to Sarah. No one did.

"Stop, Bernard," I said forcefully.

Bernard kept coming forward. Behind him, I could see a reporter talking into a microphone with the camera pointed in the house. Little Luther Pleasant was watching with excitement in his eyes. He wanted to see some action.

"Don't make me do this, Bernard," I said firmly.

Without a word, he walked toward the stairs and I stepped in front of him. Bernard swung wildly at my head and I ducked. If I didn't know him, if I didn't feel his grief, I would have seriously hurt him. Instead, I floated to his right and let him grab me. When he did, I simply twisted his wrist sharply, forcing it to do what it wasn't designed to do. It was a simple move. Didn't take much strength at all. He groaned loudly. I continued to apply pressure until Bernard went down on one knee, then the other.

"Bernard," I said. "I don't want to hurt you. But you don't want to see her that way. Believe me you don't."

With that, he broke down. Cried like a baby. I let him go so he could grieve unrestrained. I looked at him, wondering if he knew something. Everybody was a suspect as far as I was concerned. Kelly had a point. What if Sarah Lawford was somehow involved with Blake Nelson and Louis Perkins?

"Bernard," Kelly said softly. "We've got some hard questions to ask you."

Bernard stood up and we all walked into the kitchen. When he saw the melted ice cream, he broke down again.

"She bought me some butter pecan ice cream," he muttered almost incoherently, then kind of slumped into one of the kitchen chairs.

Kelly and I looked at each other. I nodded my head. She knew I was with her, knew I wanted her to grill him while I consoled. It may seem ruthless, but most of the time the killer is someone the victim knew. We had no way of knowing if Bernard knew what was going on at Norrell or not. Killing Sarah could have been a message for him.

"Do you have any idea who might want to kill Sarah?" Kelly asked as delicately as she could. I stood right next to Bernard with my hand on his shoulder.

"No. Nobody at all." Bernard sobbed. "She was the sweetest woman I've ever known."

Kelly looked at me. I could tell she didn't want to ask the next question but we had to get his reaction. As far as we knew, he could be the killer.

"Did you two have a falling-out?" Kelly asked tentatively. "We know how it is with wedding plans. Sometimes couples get scared when their wedding date nears. Did something like that happen between you two?"

"You suspect me?" Bernard asked incredulously.

"No," I interjected. "We're just doing our best to eliminate you as a suspect. We have to do it, Bernard. It's standard procedure."

"Where were you today, Bernard?" Kelly asked.

"I was at the school all evening grading papers," Bernard said. "I was trying to get ahead. You guys know the school's demanding schedule. Sarah and I can't afford to get behind. We'll never catch up."

"Anybody see you there?" Kelly asked.

"Only about twenty other teachers who are also preparing for the last break before the fall semester."

I looked at Kelly and smiled. Then I patted Bernard on the shoulder. I was genuinely happy that he had a solid alibi. At least we could verify that Bernard Rodgers didn't kill her, which also meant that maybe Sarah Lawford had nothing to do with Nelson Blake, Louis Perkins, and Norrell Prison. However, that left another nagging question. If Sarah Lawford wasn't involved with Blake and Perkins, why was she raped and murdered in the same fashion as Perkins and his wife?

Kelly's cell rang. "Hello," she said. "Oh, hi, Sterling."

She looked at me, grinned and gave me a thumbs-up sign.

# CHAPTER 31

**K**elly offered to drop Bernard Rodgers off at his mother's house. It was on her way to the Willard Intercontinental Hotel where she planned to meet Sterling Wise. As I walked out of Sarah Lawford's house, I was deluged with questions from local reporters who probably hoped to make names for themselves. Bright lights were blinding me as I forced my way through the crowd.

I stopped in my tracks when I heard an eager reporter ask, "Is there any truth to Matthew Henson's most well-liked teacher being involved with Warden Louis Perkins and Washington's drug king, Nelson Blake?"

Without thinking, I turned around and faced the reporter. The cameras were rolling. For all I knew, the feed was going out live. But it irritated the hell out of me for the accusation to be made without hard evidence. Reporters always find a sucker to bite on the information hook; especially once they learn you're personally involved. A well-liked teacher at my daughter's school was beaten with a bullwhip, raped and murdered in her own home right across the street from where I lived. Yeah, I was personally involved. So I took the bait and became the fool they were looking for. The young reporter shoved the microphone in my face, and I lit into her like there was no tomorrow.

"It's that kind of reporting that sullies people's reputations. Have you no shame, Madam? Don't you even friggin' care that her family could be watching this tonight? Sarah Lawford had parents and siblings who loved her and a fiancé she was going to marry just a few weeks from now. Do you even know if they've been notified of her gruesome and brutal murder?"

The young reporter poised herself and looked me right in the eye and said, "So, Sarah Lawford is dead? And you say her death was gruesome and brutal? I never said anything about Ms. Lawford being dead, Special Agent Phoenix Perry. You did."

I felt like a complete idiot. They had me on camera telling the world that Sarah Lawford was dead before her parents had been notified. I looked at the young reporter who was now laughing at me under her breath. The cameras were still filming. I just walked off, pushing my way through the burgeoning crowd.

As I walked across the street to my home, I could hear the reporter talking. "Perhaps Special Agent Phoenix Perry is one of the many things wrong with the Federal Bureau of Investigation. They're quick to point out the shortcomings of the media while their own house is in shambles. This is Season Chambers, WSDC News."

# CHAPTER 32

Sterling Wise opened the door to his posh suite at the Willard and saw a tall blonde with slim hips whose breasts looked like a 38-C. Giorgio perfume filled the air. He took in the fragrance and desired to smell more of it. The shapely blonde was wearing a pair of black slacks and a purple sleeveless V-neck sweater with two-toned matching flat shoes. Sterling stared for a moment, his lust ever-growing.

Kelly liked the ravenous look in his eyes. The very same look was in hers. She wanted him inside her right then, but she kept hearing Phoenix's admonitions about being loose. Her best friend had often told her she needed to be more disciplined when it came to sex. *Don't be so quick to give it up. At least wait a month or two*, Phoenix had said.

"So, you ready for a game of pool?" Kelly asked him.

"You know a place that's open this late?" Sterling asked, looking at his watch.

"Yeah. The Patriot Bar and Grill is open until two." Kelly smiled. "They make fabulous turkey sandwiches, if you're hungry."

"Let me get my wallet," Sterling said.

He walked through the suite to the bedroom where he had left his wallet on the nightstand. He picked it up and checked to see how much cash he had just in case he needed to stop in the lobby and use the ATM.

"So, counselor, are you hungry or what?" Kelly asked flirtatiously.

"Very. Are you?"

"Uh-huh."

They took the elevator to the parking lot and got into Kelly's black Stingray. She put the car in first gear and screeched out of the parking lot.

"I'm gonna take the long route. Show you the town. Okay?"

"Sure. It's your town and it's definitely your car. Do with me what you will."

"Funny you should say that because that's exactly what I planned on doing." Kelly grinned. "Mind if I ask you a personal question, counselor?"

"I don't mind. Go ahead, Agent McPherson."

"You sure?"

"I'm sure," Sterling said.

"Was there anything between you and Tiffany?

You don't have to answer, but it's been bugging the hell outta me."

Sterling smiled and looked out the window at the Lincoln Memorial as they zoomed past. "Why?"

"Just wanna know."

"Yeah, but why?"

"If I tell you why, will you still answer?"

"I might." Sterling flirted.

"Okay, but don't get mad. Tiffany was a good-looking girl. And personally, I don't see how you could resist, given all the traveling together, and the convenience of the hotels. Were you two close?"

"Tiffany and I were close, but that's it. We decided early on not to get involved sexually."

"Whose decision was that? Hers?"

"Actually, it was mine."

"Really?"

"I think you're being a little disingenuous, Agent McPherson."

"Why do you think that?" Kelly smiled.

"Honestly?" Sterling asked.

"Yes, honestly."

"I think the real reason you're skeptical about it being my decision is because Tiffany was not only good-looking, but she was white. A lot of white women think that black men want them because of some mythical ideas about forbidden fruit. Yet, at the same time, they never question the fact that women are the ones who determine if sex is going to take place. For example, if something happens between us tonight, unless I rape you, which I won't, you determine if you want to come back to my hotel, come in my room and into my bed. I have no mystical charms or potions. Women determine that. Not men."

Kelly pulled into the parking lot of the Patriot Bar and Grill, parked the Stingray, and turned off the growling engine. "Have I offended you, counselor?"

"Have you been disingenuous?"

"Yes, but I really didn't mean to." Kelly placed her hand on his. "I'm sorry, okay. But the truth is, black men come on to me all the time."

"And white men don't? Is that what you're telling me, Agent McPherson?"

"No, white men do, too."

"And why do you suppose that is?"

"Truthfully? Because I'm a fine-lookin' broad."

Sterling laughed. "The truth has finally shown itself. If white men find you attractive, why can't any man find you attractive?"

"I guess they can," Kelly said reflectively. "Does this conversation mean I can't get a little later?"

"Depends. If you win, yes."

"And if I lose?"

"Self-stimulation is always an option."

# CHAPTER 33

Two hours later Sterling and Kelly were back at the Willard. They hadn't gotten in the door good before they engaged in a deep kiss that threatened to asphyxiate both of them. Their hands pulled and tugged at each other's clothing recklessly. With her sweater off and tossed on the floor, Sterling reached around with one hand and unhooked her bra like he had done it a million times.

Kelly finished taking the bra off and tossed it near her sweater. Wantonly, hungrily, Sterling sucked her breasts while she leaned against the door of the suite.

Kelly moaned softly. "I need this."

"Do you?"

"Yes," Kelly said. "Be good to me. Be very good to me."

Sterling moved from her breasts back to her wide kissable lips and plunged in hard. He needed this, too. His body ached for a release and he would have it. While they kissed, he continued to undress her, tugging at her zipper, and almost breaking the button.

"Let me do it," Kelly said.

A few seconds later, her pants were down to her ankles. She kicked them the rest of the way off and to the side.

Sterling put his hand inside her panties and felt her bush just before he felt her liquid. She moaned when he touched her there, in her most sensitive area. Up and down, he moved his hand until her moaning became synchronized with his steady movement.

"It...feels...so...good," Kelly heard herself saying. "Don't you stop. Don't you dare stop."

Sterling continued the tease that was building, becoming volcanic with each and every stroke, threatening to erupt at any moment.

"Yes...yes...oh, yes," Kelly muttered. Her mind and body were one, like a spiritual journey to a land where pleasure is the only emotion allowed. Then suddenly, she convulsed. "Oh, my God...Oh, my God...Oh, my God."

Sterling was still lapping at her breast when her release came. Kelly pulled his head in and almost smothered him. She couldn't help herself. His head was the only thing she had to hang on to.

"I want you in me now," she practically screamed. "Right now."

"Let me get a rubber," Sterling panted.

"Hurry up! Shit! I'm ready!"

Sterling went into the bedroom to get a condom but before he had a chance to return, Kelly had kicked off her panties and followed him. She pushed him onto the bed, unbuckled his pants, and slid them down along with his underwear. She took the condom out of his hand, opened it, and put it in her mouth. Then using her mouth, she put the condom on his erect penis.

"You like that?" she asked just before straddling him. "I saw that on one of the HBO *Real Sex* episodes."

"Really, Agent McPherson? Does the bureau know your viewing habits?"

"Of course. It's required. Now, be quiet and let me get my swerve on."

# CHAPTER 34

My phone rang loudly, waking me and my husband out of a deep death-like sleep at two a.m. Keyth answered the phone and handed it to me.

"Who is it? Kelly?"

"No. It's your new boss."

"Hello," I said groggily.

"Agent Perry, this is Acting Director Malone. I thought you were on extended vacation."

"I am," I said, still out of it, eyes still closed.

"Then what the hell did you think you were doing going on television speaking for the bureau?"

That got my attention real quick. My eyes shot open and wide. I knew Kortney was going to find out soon enough. But not at two o'clock in the morning. I felt like a kid who knew he was going to be punished for missing curfew so he stays out even longer. The kid realizes the punishment will be the same regardless of how late he returns.

So flippantly, I said, "Kortney, it's late and my husband has to get up early. I would appreciate it if you called during normal business hours."

She was silent. We had been at the Academy together so I knew what she was doing, knew how she thought. Whenever she was about to blow up, she simply silenced herself, which was exactly what I wanted her to do. At least I'd be able to sleep the rest of the night. If she was really hard-up, she could force me to meet her at the bureau where I'd get the tongue-lashing of my life. But by pissing her off, she would think first.

"Agent Perry," Kortney finally said after a long pause. "I apologize for calling your home at this hour, but I'm looking at this idiot who looks just like you in an FBI windbreaker on the news. Give me one reason why I shouldn't suspend you on the spot."

"Kortney, I screwed up," I said, changing my tone. "I let my emotions get the better of me. I knew the victim. She was one of my daughter's teachers."

"I'm sorry, Phoenix." Kortney softened a bit. "But was the reporter right? Did the victim have anything to do with the Perkins murders?"

"I don't believe she did. No," I said sincerely.

"You're absolutely sure about that?"

"Yes," I said confidently.

"And you know that because..." Kortney's words trailed off.

I paused. I had fallen into yet another trap. Kortney had set me up. I felt about as bright as a two-dollar whore bragging about giving change back to her customers. Both the reporter and Kortney had used my emotions against me in subtle ways to elicit truth from me that I, under normal circumstances, would have never divulged. The reporter saw my white-hot anger and knew immediately that I would want to set the record straight. Now Kortney was pulling my loyalty strings to siphon off information. *Pimped twice in one night.*

"Well?" Kortney said. "How do you know, Phoenix?"

"Well...I guess I really don't know."

"And that's why you keep your damn mouth closed in front of the media. Do you realize your emotional outburst made the national broadcast? The local affiliate notified the network and now CNN has it. It's being replayed every half-hour on *Headline News.*"

I remained silent.

"Tell me something, Phoenix. How much did your house cost?"

"Huh?" *Where did that come from?*

"Humor me. How much did your house cost?"

"That's personal, Kortney," I said. I didn't want people in the bureau knowing how much money my father and husband's private investigation firm was pulling in.

"You know I can easily find out, Phoenix. It's a matter of public record. But if I did that, I would have to wait until tomorrow to make my salient point. Now, how much did you pay for your house?"

"Four hundred fifty thousand," I said. If we lived just about anywhere else in the country, with the exception of Los Angeles and New York, our home would be a palace. But in Arlington, houses are very expensive. It would be difficult to find a decent house for less than $230,000. That is, if you want more than one bathroom.

"That's what I figured," Kortney said with a satisfied tone. "Now, how is it that a teacher can afford to live right across the street from you?"

"She inherited the money from her deceased uncle," I said matter-of-factly.

"Are you shark sure?"

I remembered the first time I heard her little euphemism, "shark sure." We were at the Academy with other would-be FBI agents practicing how to go through doors. Kortney and I had gone through a door and yelled "clear." We heard an instructor say, "Bang! Bang! Both of you are dead." Then he reminded us to look behind the door. Later, at mealtime, Kortney had said she would be shark sure the next time she yelled "clear." We all laughed hysterically. We knew what she meant, but it was funny as hell.

"Yes."

"Well you better be shark sure, Phoenix. Shark sure!"

I remained quiet. I was thinking about what Kortney was saying. What if Sarah Lawford lied about the inheritance money? If she lied, that in and of itself would not prove that she was involved with Warden Perkins. But it would raise questions. Questions that could prove to be embarrassing for me and the bureau. I was the one who had vouched for her on television a few hours earlier.

"You know the media is going to ask some of the same questions that I'm asking, Phoenix."

"I know," I said, shaking my head. All of a sudden, I wasn't so sure about Sarah Lawford. I wasn't sure at all. If we couldn't prove that she inherited a substantial amount of money, the media was going to have a field day.

"Listen, you can pretend to be on an extended vacation if you want, but I'm putting you back on pay status, which means I expect regular reports from you and McPherson. You don't have to come into the office, but you do have to report your findings to me. Agreed?"

"Agreed," I said.

"Apologize to Keyth for me. Goodnight."

# CHAPTER 35

Alex and Sam were sitting in a black Oldsmobile parked a few hundred feet from Taylor and Jack Hoffman's multimillion-dollar residence in the Rosemont district of Alexandria, Virginia. The white painted brick colonial was distinguished from the other homes by four huge columns that stood in front of the entrance. A red brick wall separated by an iron gate surrounded the property.

The twins had followed Taylor Hoffman to Dulles International Airport, where she dropped off her husband who had taken the last flight out to Los Angeles. They had waited in the sweltering August heat for Taylor Hoffman to turn off the only light burning in her bedroom. It was so hot that they had discussed turning the air conditioning on, but decided against it. They were taking a big chance as it was. If someone heard a car start, they might look outside and see them. Maybe even call the police.

The Hoffmans were an upwardly mobile couple with everything to look forward to. The young couple was married in June, a few weeks after twenty-six-year-old Taylor had graduated from Georgetown University, where she earned her degree in corporate law. Earlier that morning, Taylor had interviewed for and accepted a coveted position with Talley, McNearney and Associates. The firm had promised her plenty of opportunities for advancement and a possible partnership if she worked hard.

Jack Hoffman had developed a virtual reality program at the Massachusetts Institute for Technology that was specifically designed for the motion picture industry's science fiction films. The program broke new ground and allowed pictures like *The Matrix* and *Titanic* to be more realistic. Jack had just accepted a three-picture deal with Paramount Pictures and was flying out to Los Angeles to begin work on a project. He had planned to leave earlier, but when Taylor landed the job at Talley, McNearney and Associates, he took a later flight so they could celebrate.

Alex was wearing a pair of headphones that were connected to a parabolic mic that was capable of picking up sound inside Taylor's bedroom. A few minutes after she turned off the light, soft snoring could be heard. The twins got out of the car and walked between the columns to the front door—duffel bag in tow. Using an alarm decoder and a set of master keys, the twins easily walked into the dark colonial without detection. They donned a pair of night vision goggles and welcomed the air-conditioned chill.

Furtively, they climbed the carpeted circular stairs and found Taylor Hoffman in the master bedroom. She was curled in a ball sound asleep under a comforter. Alex took off the goggles, sat on the bed without disturbing her, and turned on the bright nightstand light.

"Taylor," Alex said, shaking her. "Wake up."

Taylor opened her eyes and was blinded momentarily by the bright light. When she was able to focus and saw who was in her house, she opened her mouth to scream, but it was too late.

Alex taped her mouth shut and smiled. "Heather Connelly, Sandra Rhodes, and Paula Stevens are dead. You didn't think we'd forget about you, did you?"

# CHAPTER 36

Early the next morning, Kelly McPherson came over to pick me up. I got into the passenger side of the Stingray. We were going to Norrell Prison to interview Salaam Khan. Kelly looked relaxed and well-rested, like she'd had her bell rung several times during the night. She hadn't looked this cheerful in over a month. I welcomed the change—even if it was due to illicit sex.

Kelly hummed as she drove down Continental Boulevard. The strange thing about it was I don't think she even realized she was humming. All I could think of was poor Sterling. She probably rode him like a wild colt in need of just the right sort of rider to bring him into submission to the bridle in his mouth. I laughed a little under my breath.

"What, Phoenix?" Kelly said, smiling widely.

I said, "Somebody got their swerve on something fierce."

"I sure did," Kelly acknowledged. "Might have to get some more before he leaves town."

I shook my head.

"So, did you howl the way you howled when we were in St. Thomas last month?" After I said that, I realized it might be a sore spot for my friend. The guy she was with at the time had betrayed her and wasn't exactly what he claimed to be. "I'm sorry, Kelly."

"Don't worry about it," she said without a change in expression.

"Musta been good," I quipped.

"Real good."

"Your first brotha?"

She smiled. "Why? Would it bother you if it wasn't?"

"Nope."

"Then, yeah. It was."

I wanted to ask her a thousand questions, but I didn't. I wanted to know why she had suddenly chosen to step over the color line. Not that it mattered. I was just curious. I wondered if it was something she had always wanted to do, but never ventured out until then. My friend seemed to like a lot of black culture, black music, black lingo. Maybe that's why we're best friends. But if I asked her why, it might put her in an awkward position and strain our relationship. And that's the last thing I wanted. So, I decided to leave it alone. What relevance did it have anyway?

"Guess who called me last night," I said, changing the subject.

"Who?"

"Kortney Malone."

Kelly frowned. "What the hell did she want?"

"Did you see *Headline News* this morning?" I asked.

"No. What did I miss?"

"When we left Sarah's house, Season Chambers set me up good. She asked me if Sarah was involved with Perkins and Blake. And you know how misleading questions like that piss me off."

Kelly nodded. "Phoenix, what did you say?"

"I said something about Sarah's murder being brutal. Asked her if she even knew if her family had been notified. That's when she dropped the hammer on me. Told me that she didn't mention anything about Sarah being dead."

"What?"

"Yep. I had told everybody that Sarah Lawford was dead before her family had been notified. Right there on television. Live and in color."

"So Kortney called to chew you out?"

"Yeah, but I handcuffed her before she had the chance. Made her behave by mentioning the late-ness of the hour. You know how Southerners are about being courteous."

"What did she do? Get quiet?"

"Yep. Then she called me off vacation and told me to report to her."

"Kinda dodged a bullet, huh?"

"Yep."

# CHAPTER 37

Norrell Prison, built in 1920, looked like a castle. It was surrounded by fifty foot walls made of gray cement. I could see armed guards in the towers that overlooked the courtyard. We got out the Stingray and started the long trek to the entrance. As we walked, we discussed the Sarah Lawford case.

"What do you think the bullwhip is all about, Phoenix?" Kelly asked. "Is it strictly for punishment? Or does he get some sort of sick sexual pleasure from it?"

"I'm not sure what to think, Kelly. If he was getting sexual pleasure from the whipping, why rape the women?"

"Humiliation?" She paused. "It could also be another form of violence."

"Hmmmm. Maybe he thinks the victims should be humbled before they're punished," I said. "If that's true, why the chain saw? That would be the third form of violence committed by the killer."

"So you think the murders could be some kinda ritual that involves the number three in some way?"

"At this point, we can't rule out anything," I said. We finally reached the gate. The guard asked us for ID. We showed her our credentials and she told us to follow the yellow arrows to the captain of the guards' office, where we would have to surrender our firearms. I heard the door slam shut behind us. There was such finality to the sound of it closing. Suddenly I was glad I was only visiting.

"Kelly," I said. "I think we would be better off not trying to figure out his ritualistic reasoning. Right now, we're just guessing. We don't have anything solid. Once we get a look at the forensics report, we'll have something to go on. But for now, we're at his mercy. He gets to go on killing until we gather enough facts to lead us to an arrest."

"Don't cha just love crime-fighting?" Kelly asked sarcastically. "We won't be able to stop this bastard until he's killed more innocent women."

The yellow arrows led us through a set of depressing gray painted corridors. We saw an inmate dressed in gray dungarees mopping the floor. He stopped working for a second and stared at us lustfully.

"Hi, lover," Kelly flirted. "We're looking for the captain of the guards' office. Are we going the right way?"

The man smiled broadly. "Yeah. Captain Callahan's office is right around the corner."

I whispered. "You can't help yourself, can you?"

"Nope. I love men, Phoenix. I like the way they look at me. Makes me feel sexy and desirable. Tell me you don't like the way men look at you."

I remained quiet. What woman doesn't want to be thought of as beautiful and desirable by the opposite sex? We turned the corner and saw Callahan's office. The door was open. Callahan was just hanging up the phone. He had a scowl on his face, and didn't bother to stand up. He just sat in his leather swivel chair, frowning at us, rocking in a slow deliberate cadence.

"Agents Perry and McPherson to see Salaam Khan."

"Let's see some ID," Callahan barked.

"Having a bad day, Captain?" Kelly smiled. "That tends to happen when you get caught distributing drugs."

Callahan stood and walked around to the front of his desk. "For the last time, produce some ID, or get the hell outta my prison!"

We whipped out our credentials. He took them out of our hands and stared at them for what seemed like five minutes. "Put your firearms on the desk."

We complied.

"Let me tell you two something," Callahan said,

staring at Kelly. "I don't give a damn what you heard. None of my officers had anything to do with the warden's death. That had to be somebody else. It wasn't us."

"So then you're admitting you did the warden's wife," Kelly quipped.

I laughed. Kelly had a way of getting on people's nerves quickly. It was a gift. She could turn a man on or off instantly with a few choice words just to get his reaction.

"You fucking bitch!" Callahan blared.

"And...loving it." Kelly smiled. "Let me tell you something, Mr. Captain of the Guards. This is a federal investigation. You don't tell us what to do. We tell you. Now, get Salaam Khan and we might not lock you up in your own prison for impeding the pursuit of justice."

Callahan picked up his phone and hit a button. "Send prisoner number 32569645 to my office immediately."

# CHAPTER 38

Salaam Khan entered Captain Callahan's office ten minutes later. I was reading his file. His name used to be Dwight Valentine. He was five nine, solidly built and clean-shaven. Looking at the photo the police took of him when he was arrested, you wouldn't be able to recognize him today. He was wearing a wet-looking curl in the photo. Now his hair was short and neatly trimmed. I could tell by the way he stood in the doorway, chest out, shoulders back, that he was a very proud man. He had educated himself, earning a master's degree in world history and another in sociology. If ever a man had reformed himself, this man had.

After serving four years of a twenty-year sentence, Valentine changed his name though he never converted to Islam. Khan had been a former pimp, but was in for felony murder. He had been strung out on heroin and foolishly agreed to drive the car during a jewelry store heist. The manager sounded the alarm and was killed. Although Khan hadn't killed anyone, being involved earned him twenty years at Norrell.

"Captain," I said. "We need to speak to Mr. Khan alone. May we use your office?"

Callahan nodded. As he walked past Kelly, he frowned. It always amazes me how effective the good cop-bad cop ploy works on just about everybody, even cops.

"Have a seat, Mr. Khan," I said, showing him genuine respect. "Looking at your record, I admire what you've done for yourself."

"Thank you," he said. "What's this all about? They tell me you two ladies are FBI agents."

He looked Kelly up and down as if he were sizing her up and smirked almost unnoticeably.

"What?" Kelly smiled.

"Sure you wanna know, Ma'am?"

"Yeah."

"No offense, but a few years ago, I would've had you working for me. Man is still so lost that he would reach deep in his pockets for a gem like you. I'm just glad I've put that life behind me."

"I'm glad you did, too." Kelly laughed. "I might have taken you up on the offer."

I cleared my throat. Kelly's personality is usually flirtatious and jovial. That's one reason I like her.

I would have taken Salaam Khan's reflective words as an insult. Kelly just goes with the flow.

"Mr. Khan," I began. "Nelson Blake told us that you would be the man to talk to about the warden's murder. What can you tell us?"

"I can tell you that Norrell Prison is a haven for criminal activity, not a penal institution. Even now, with all the heat of the investigation into the warden's murder, it's still business as usual here."

"What do you mean?" I asked.

"I mean the gangs still run the prison because none of the guards have been removed. They no longer have a lab, but drugs are still coming in. The place is still a cash cow. And when all of this blows over, they'll set the lab back up. The prisoners will be singing "Happy Days Are Here Again." "

I frowned. I thought it strange that not much had changed, but I wasn't there to fix the problem at Norrell. I was there to solve a couple of murders. "Who had the most to gain from the death of Warden Perkins?"

"Captain Terry Callahan. Word on the wire is that he was sexin' the warden's wife. The warden found out about it and confronted him. Callahan didn't bother to deny it. He even told Perkins that if he wanted him to stop bangin' his wife, he wanted a bigger cut. Truth is, Callahan is the one who

KEITH LEE JOHNSON

brought the warden in on the deal with Nelson Blake. Blake and I are best friends. Grew up together. He used to visit me before all this began. At the time, Callahan was being squeezed by his ex-wife. He's got alimony and child support payments that all but wipe out the check he makes."

"Are you concerned for your life?" Kelly asked.

"No. Most of this stuff is going to come out anyway. Plus Blake won't allow anything to happen to me. Even if something did happen to me, somebody needs to shut Little Babylon down."

"How does Sarah Lawford tie into this?" I asked.

"Who?" Salaam questioned.

My cell rang. "Excuse me a second. Agent Perry."

"Phoenix, this is Kortney Malone. Get over to 1169 Cobblestone Drive. Senator Hoffman's daughter-in-law has been murdered. Same MO as the warden and Sarah Lawford."

# CHAPTER 39

Season Chambers was in front of the Hoffman house giving a live report when Kelly and I arrived. Our eyes met as we drove past. Season smiled triumphantly. I felt my temper starting to flare up. I didn't like being made a fool of. Truth be told, I had done it to myself. I could have simply said "no comment" and walked across the street. But I had to open my mouth and insert both my feet.

There were so many bureau cars, police vehicles, and media vans in front of the house that we had to park nearly a block away. It was too hot for our FBI windbreakers so we displayed our credentials on our belts and walked toward the Hoffman house.

Season Chambers had just finished her report when we got to the house. She came over to me. I expected her to be as conniving as she was the night before at Sarah Lawford's place, but she wasn't. She was a totally different person. No claws. No fangs.

Perhaps I misjudged the young reporter when she smiled at me. But still, I couldn't help being suspicious.

"Agent Perry," Season began. "I apologize for what I did to you last night. That was unnecessary and it was wrong. You had just seen the remains of your neighbor and I ambushed you on live television. Can you forgive me?"

Skeptical, I looked at her. My incredulity was unmistakable, I'm sure. "Why the sudden change of tactics?" I asked.

"Because this is the third woman who has been raped and mutilated," Season said. "We've got a bonafide serial killer out there. No woman is safe."

"Three? Is there a woman I don't know about?" I asked Season. I didn't tell her that Sarah had been number two. But someone had. The last thing we needed was for reporters to know that there had been three women killed in the D.C. area with the same MO.

"C'mon, Agent Perry," Season said dryly. "I have my sources. I know what happened to Kathy Perkins and Sarah Lawford. I also know what happened to Taylor Hoffman. Do you really think the murder of a senator's daughter-in-law is not going to get out?"

"What do you want, Ms. Chambers?" Kelly asked.

"Just to help in any way I can," Season replied.

"Fine," I said. "If we think of a way that you can help, we'll let you know."

I was troubled by what I saw when I walked into the Hoffmans' bedroom. Detective McDonald and his team were already collecting evidence when I said, "Stop what you're doing. The bureau is taking over from here."

# CHAPTER 40

First, I saw the usual looks of disdain that accompanied any hostile takeover like this. The attitude of DCPD was typical. They hated when we took over an investigation in progress, especially when they knew we would probably need them later. McDonald glared at me as he and his homicide team left the area. I mouthed, "Sorry."

This crime was different, yet it was the same. I noticed right away that there were blood patterns splattered on the walls. It looked like the victim's extremities were thrown against them.

"What do you think, Kelly?" I asked.

"Whoever did this was pissed, Phoenix."

"I was thinking the same thing," I said. "I'm wondering where Terry Callahan was last night. And could he have committed this crime to cover the others? This is the only one to have these kinds of blood stains, Kelly."

"I know," she said.

"Is it possible that we have two different killers? Two killers, killing the exact same way. Yet, not exactly the same? Raping, whipping, and mutilating? It doesn't make any sense."

"None at all," Kelly said.

I walked around the room, taking in everything, looking for anything out of the ordinary. Other than the mutilated body of Taylor Hoffman, nothing seemed to be missing or out of place that I could tell. I walked over to the mirrored dresser. There was a wedding picture of Taylor and her husband, I presumed.

"Where's the husband?" I called out to the officer guarding the door.

"We don't know," he answered.

"Kelly, let's get Senator Hoffman on the phone. Maybe he knows where the husband is."

"The senator just arrived," the officer told us.

"Officer, radio downstairs and have him wait in the living room or something," I said.

"I'll find out what he knows, Phoenix," Kelly said.

I nodded and continued looking around the room as I put on a pair of surgical gloves. How did he get in? There was no sign of forced entry. Did she let him in? I reasoned. If she did, it had to be someone she knew. Why else would she open the door in her pajamas?

There was a phone on the nightstand. Maybe that could tell me something. I could see whom she talked to last. Maybe the alarm did go off and he forced her to call the security company. I hit the redial button. The liquid crystal screen read local weather. That didn't mean she didn't call the security company. She could have used another phone in the house to call them. I hit the directory button on the phone and found the number to the security company. I dialed them on my cell.

"Alexandria Security. Mary Ann speaking. May I help you?"

"This is Special Agent in Charge, Phoenix Perry," I said, trying to sound official. The person who answered the phone could very easily blow me off and not answer any of my questions. So, I wanted to sound important. I could easily subpoena the record, but I wanted an answer immediately. "I'm calling from the home of one of your clients, and I need to know if Taylor Hoffman, who lives at 1169 Cobblestone Drive, called in an inadvertent alarm last night?"

"Just a moment, Special Agent Perry." I could hear the woman hitting keys in the background.

"No. No one from that address called in last night," Mary Ann said. "As a matter of fact, there hasn't been an inadvertent alarm at that residence since June, Ma'am."

"Thank you," I said and hung up. "Officer, call downstairs and find out if the alarm is off."

Taylor Hoffman may not have turned the alarm system on. For all I knew, they may not have even used the system.

"It's off, Agent Perry," the officer said.

"Thanks," I said and continued scouring the room for clues. I opened the drawer on the nightstand. A tablet and pencil were in there.

One of our people from the crime lab put on a pair of ultraviolet goggles and looked at the bed. "Semen," he said excitedly and collected a sample.

I opened the other nightstand drawer and found an autographed copy of Bebe Moore Campbell's *Brothers and Sisters*. I went back to the mirrored dresser and began opening drawers one at a time. Nothing unusual. Underwear. Folded clothing. I didn't know what I was looking for, so I lifted up the clothing, which yielded nothing until I opened the bottom drawer on the right.

That drawer contained all sorts of sex toys ranging from a video from the Sinclair Institute that read *32 Ways to Love Your Lover* to a Kegelcisor to assorted dildos, lubricants, edible panties, cock rings, and flavored condoms. Taylor was a freak, I thought. I didn't mean to. It just came to mind without effort.

"The husband's in Los Angeles working on a science fiction film, Phoenix," Kelly said. "He had to be there today and had planned to leave earlier yesterday. But Taylor Hoffman had just gotten hired at a prestigious law firm here in Alexandria and they celebrated. That's why the husband left so late last night."

"Hence the semen on the bed," I said.

"Huh?"

"Crime lab found semen on the sheets. I'm betting it's the husband's and not the killer's. What time did the husband leave last night?"

"Twelve-thirty this morning."

I called headquarters to confirm that the husband was actually on the flight. "This is Agent Perry. Check the flight manifests on all flights leaving Washington last night for Los Angeles. Tell me if you find Jack Hoffman on any of them."

"Do you spell that with two F's or one?" the tech asked.

"Two, I think.

"Yes," the tech said. "Departed Dulles at twelve-thirty. Arrived LAX at two-thirty Pacific."

"Thanks," I said. "That clears the husband."

"Nice crib," Kelly said. "Rich folks got it made. Would you believe this house is a wedding present from Senator Hoffman, Phoenix? That's right. A

2.2 million-dollar house. For a friggin' wedding present. If I could only be so lucky. I might have to marry Sterling and live good for a change. He's got bucks and makin' more all the time."

I shook my head and laughed. "You're crazy, girl."

# CHAPTER 41

I briefed Kortney Malone on the evidence found at the Hoffman house. When she asked me where Kelly was, I told her that Kelly was running down a lead, but actually, she had made plans to meet Sterling at his hotel. We didn't have much on the killer and we had put in a full day. Why not let Kelly have a little fun, I thought.

Kortney didn't question my veracity so I went on to explain that Salaam Khan had told us that he thought Terry Callahan had killed the warden and his wife, but he had no idea who Sarah Lawford was. That didn't mean that he didn't do both crimes. I went on to tell her that whoever killed the Perkins and Sarah may not have killed Taylor Hoffman. That one may have been a copy-cat. If Terry Callahan was involved, he could have had one of his officers do the murder.

After I finished my report to Kortney, I went to the crime lab. The criminalist assigned to the case was Karl McGregor. He collected the evidence at the Perkins and Sarah Lawford murder scenes.

"What do you have for me, McGregor?" I asked.

"The Perkins and Lawford murders were committed by the same man, Phoenix," he said.

"You absolutely sure about that?"

"No doubt at all," McGregor said, looking over his spectacles. He handed me a specimen in a glass vial.

"What's this?"

"It's kangaroo hide. It took me a while to trace it, Phoenix. Originally, I assumed it was cowhide. That's why the first rule in forensics is don't assume anything. It's also the easiest rule to break. Some things look obvious, but they're far from it."

"Okay, I'll bite. What's the difference?" I asked.

"Kangaroo hide is ten times stronger, Phoenix," McGregor said. "Whoever this guy is, he wanted to inflict some serious pain. I traced this particular kangaroo hide to Australia, believe it or not."

"So what are you saying? Crocodile Dundee is running around D.C. whipping and hacking up women?"

"No, I'm saying that the man that used the whip is very particular about his tools. He'll more than likely be that way about everything. His lifestyle, his dress, his manner, his victims, everything."

"How'd you find the whip?"

"Found it on the Internet. The whip is called a Tornado. It's hand-made by a man named Si Davey. Called him a little while ago. He told me he sent three to the post office on Pennsylvania Avenue, PO Box 12666. He didn't have a name. The customer paid with an international money order."

"Great work, McGregor," I almost screamed. It was six-thirty. The post office was closed. We'd get over there first thing in the morning.

# CHAPTER 42

"Mommy! Savannah shouted when she saw me. I picked her up and held her tight. "What's for dinner?" I asked. "It smells wonderful."

"Grandma cooked some greens, sweet potatoes and roast beef before she left." Savannah smiled. "The sweet cornbread is almost done, too. I'm starvin'. You?"

"Yeah. Let's go eat."

"I'll race you, Mommy."

"Ready, set, go!" I shouted and let the flesh of my flesh beat me to the dinner table. "Keyth?"

"Hold on for a second, baby," he shouted from the family room. "I'm watching ESPN."

"Okay!" I yelled back. "We're setting the table."

"I'll be right in," Keyth said.

Savannah opened the silverware drawer and pulled out the eating utensils. I opened the cabinet above the sink and pulled out plates and drinking glasses.

"What are we drinking with dinner, Mommy?"

"Hawaiian Punch. Or iced tea. You choose," I said.

"Uhhh, let me see," Savannah said, then opened the refrigerator. "I gotta taste for iced tea!"

My daughter sounded just like my father. That's exactly how he used to say he wanted tea. For a moment, my heart ached. It had been a little over a month since he was killed. Sometimes I wondered if I'd ever get over it. For years, it had been just me and my father. My mother had died giving birth to me. My father and I were more than close, more than father and daughter. My father was my friend, my confidant, and my trusted advisor.

I remember when I told him that I liked a Chinese boy who I studied Kung Fu with. His name was Ze Quan Lo, my master's son. I called him Quan. We were both fifteen years old. It's funny now, but in the beginning of our training, when we were eight, we didn't like each other. We competed to gain the favor of his father, Master Ying Ming Lo. My father had told me that when you hate someone that much, deep down, you really like them. Otherwise, you wouldn't be so consumed by your emotions. I honestly don't know when it happened, but sometime during the summer, not too long after my birthday, we both realized how much we liked each other.

"Mommy! Snap out of it!" Savannah laughed.

"Huh?" I said.

"You were daydreaming, Mommy."

"I was just thinking of your grandfather and my first boyfriend."

"Boyfriend?" Keyth chimed in after walking into the kitchen. "You told me I made you forget every man you had ever dated."

I laughed. "You did. But from time to time, something reminds me of Daddy. We spent twelve years in China. It's difficult not to think of my Chinese family when I think of my daddy."

"I know, baby," Keyth said.

My eyes welled with water. Eventually my heart won't ache; the tears won't leave their tracks when I think of him. Keyth put his arms around me. Savannah put her arms around both of us. I wept. I love my family so much. I'm just so grateful.

"It's all right, Mommy. When you die, I'll cry when I think about how much I miss you, too, okay?"

We laughed.

"Y'all ready to eat?" Keyth asked.

My husband and Savannah finished setting the table while I put the sweet potatoes in the microwave.

"Guess who got into a fight today?" Keyth asked.

By the tone in his voice, I knew it was Savannah. She had earned her green sash, which is a far cry from being a black sash. Nevertheless, green is two levels up from white, it's high enough to seriously hurt someone. I stared at my daughter, waiting for her to explain.

"Don't worry, Mommy." She smiled. "I didn't kill 'em."

"Savannah, you know better than to be fighting," I said.

"I know, but they were picking on Luther," she said. "They push him around all the time. And you told me that I could use the art to defend myself and other people, too."

I had told her that. And I meant it. "Luther Pleasant?"

"Yep."

"So what happened?" I asked, and started my dinner.

"I told them to leave Luther alone, or else."

"And?"

"They chose else."

"How many boys were there?" I asked.

"Two. But they weren't boys; they were girls."

"Girls? Bullying Luther?" I heard myself ask. "He's forever asking me to teach him. I guess I better start training him."

# CHAPTER 43

Three bullwhips! I was taking a shower when it hit me that McGregor had said that three bullwhips had come from Australia. Was the killer a collector? Or was he afraid they might somehow break, or lose their effectiveness? I couldn't shake the feeling that the bullwhips were a big piece of the puzzle. A few other things puzzled me, too. Were all of the victims tied into Norrell Prison and the drug connection? Why were some of the victims' extremities thrown against the wall while others were not?

The post office had to keep some sort of records on whom they rented boxes to. They probably had an address. Maybe even a phone number. We were close to solving this thing. I was sure of it. That's how it is with cases. Nothing makes sense until you find a clue that turns out to be the linchpin on which all other parts hang.

"Phoenix," I heard Keyth yell over the splashing

water. "There's a Detective Thompson on the phone from Malibu."

I stepped out of the shower. My husband looked at my nude body and smiled in such a way that I knew we were going to do it. I wrapped myself in a red beach towel and teasingly squeezed my husband's erection as I sauntered past him.

"You know when you get off the phone, we gon' have to take care of a little business." Keyth beamed. "Brotha feelin' like Marvin Gaye. Need a little sexual healing."

We kissed. "You gon' be able to handle it?" I asked him.

"Are you?" Keyth asked.

"We'll see, won't we?" I said, then went into the bedroom. I sat on the bed, put the phone to my ear, and rested it on my shoulder while I put lotion on my body. "Agent Perry."

"Agent Perry, Steven Thompson here. I'm a detective with the Malibu Police Department. Your people patched me through to your home. I apologize for calling you at this hour, but I have some pertinent information for you."

Keyth had begun to massage my hard nipples and I felt myself sliding down that slippery slope to ecstasy. His hands were the masters of my body's sensuality. They felt so good, so erotic, yet sensitive and strong. I couldn't help responding to them.

"Pertinent to what, detective?"

Keyth's hand had found its way to my moist crotch, touching my sensitive spot. I let my neck fall back as I gave into my body's beckoning.

"Pertinent to the three murders you're working on. A few days ago, we got a 911 call, but no one was on the other end. We sent a squad car to the residence and found a bloodbath. Three women had been beaten with a bullwhip and dismembered with a chain saw."

When Detective Thompson said that, I felt like I had just been awakened with ice cold water. I removed Keyth's hand from my crotch and sat on the edge of the bed.

"What?" I said in horror.

"Three of them, Agent Perry. Now you've got three. What's interesting is, we found three men dead at the bottom of the bluff right behind the mansion. And get this: one of the three men, Jasper Hunter, had had sex with one of the murder victims. Her name was Paula Stevens. Apparently they were having a serious fuck festival."

"Why do you say that, detective?"

"Because the coroner found traces of Sandra Rhodes' vaginal secretion on one of the victims' tongues. The trace evidence shows pool chalk and green felt material on Sandra Rhodes' clothing and on her ass. It looks like Heather Connelly was performing cunnilingus on Sandra while her live-in boyfriend Jasper Hunter was bangin' Paula Stevens. Her vaginal liquid was on his penis. We found carpet fibers on both knees. The killer must have walked in unexpectedly and it was another Helter Skelter. Blood was splattered on the walls from the body parts being thrown against it. Weird as hell, Agent Perry."

"Yes, it is. Here in D.C., it's the same and it's different. It's like the killer is angry with some of the victims and not angry with others. Almost as if they're two different killers. Maybe one is a copycat."

"Maybe. Another thing. The bullwhip that the perp used came from Australia. It's made of..."

"Kangaroo hide," I finished his sentence.

"Yeah. Must be an Aussie."

"Not necessarily, Detective. The killer purchased the bullwhips on the Internet and had them shipped to a PO box at one of our local post offices. My partner and I are going to check it out in the morning."

"What the hell is going on?" Thompson asked.

"I don't know, Detective. I just know that women are being beaten with a bullwhip and dismembered."

"Yeah. But why aren't the men being whipped and dismembered?" Thompson asked.

"Only one man killed here so far. And he was beaten with the whip," I told him.

"I've got three murdered men who weren't beaten."

"This is getting more and more weird," I said.

"I couldn't agree with you more."

"Detective, I sure would like to get a look at that crime scene."

"I can fax you photos and a copy of everything we have if you like."

"I like."

Before hanging up, I gave Thompson the fax number and my home phone number just in case he thought of something else. I also gave him my email address so I could see colored photos of the victims.

I found myself asking more questions. Why kill Louis and Kathy Perkins in Washington, kill six more people in Malibu, then return to Washington, and kill again? Why didn't he kill all of the D.C. victims before going to Malibu?

I was ready to pick up where Keyth and I had left off. I turned around and he was fast asleep. I kind of laughed and shook my head. He'd gotten me all steamed up. There was a bit of a blaze between my legs and now he couldn't hose me down.

# CHAPTER 44

The fax machine was printing when I entered my office. Several sheets of the coroner's report were already in the printer carriage. I sat down in my black leather chair, and then began reading the pages as they came out.

The killer was extremely efficient. No trace evidence, no footprints in the Malibu sand, no sperm, not even a pubic hair was found on the scene. That was encouraging because that was exactly what we had. Victims and no idea who committed the crimes. Therefore, it was a foregone conclusion that the FBI, the Malibu and the D.C. police departments were all looking for the same man.

I hit the power button on my computer and continued reading the report while the computer warmed up. My desktop was a picture of Wesley Snipes in his outfit as the vampire hunter: Blade.

Snipes was wearing dark shades, sporting a tight fade with circular tattoos on his head. Soon, small icons materialized on my desktop. I clicked on the America Online icon and continued reading while it loaded.

The coroner believed that a woman named Heather Connelly was the first to die the night of July 29. I frowned. That was the night before we came home from Universal City. I shook that coincidence off and signed on to America Online. A few seconds letter, I heard the software say, "You've got mail!"

I clicked on the mail icon and saw the e-mail from Detective Thompson. I double-clicked on the mail he'd sent and it opened. Then I began downloading the photos onto my desktop so I could look at them without having to load the America Online software. As the photos downloaded, I continued reading.

I was thinking, blah, blah, blah, blah, as I read. I had already known everything the coroner had written. We had fresh stiffs of our own. But I continued reading anyway. Then I found myself smiling. The Malibu coroner concluded that either the killer was ambidextrous, or there were two killers at the Connelly mansion that night. One left-handed. The other right-handed. This was huge.

I could hardly contain myself. We finally had something.

I had read the coroner's report of the Perkins murders but the Lawford and Hoffman autopsies hadn't been available. I hadn't pushed for it since we knew they had been cut to pieces while they were still alive. Now I wanted to know if there was more than one killer in Washington. I was almost sure there was. But what was the motive?

The Malibu coroner found massive amounts of cocaine in Heather Connelly's system. None in Paula Stevens. None in Sandra Rhodes. None in the men found at the bottom of the bluffs. Maybe it was about drugs. Maybe Heather Connelly was the ringleader in Malibu. Why not? Somebody had to be supplying the Hollywood crowd. Why not Heather Connelly? As far as I'm concerned, anything goes in Malibu, Beverly Hills, and Hollywood. It's like Babylon out there.

"Files done!" the America Online software announced.

I put the report on my desk and opened the photos. Under the icon of the first picture were the words Connelly Mansion. I opened it. The grounds leading up to the mansion were pristine—the lawn manicured. I could see red, white, and yellow roses just outside the front door. The next icon read: garage. I opened it and saw a photo of a thir-teen-car garage. All the doors were open and I saw expensive luxury cars. Small drops of oil were visible in a couple of empty spaces where cars must have been.

The next series of icons read autopsy photos, back, arms, legs, torso, head, breasts, and vagina, in that order. I took a deep breath and exhaled. For a second or two, I wasn't going to open any of the pictures. What was the point? I asked myself. I had seen the bodies of Sarah Lawford and Taylor Hoffman. Why torture myself? Incentive. Coco Nimburu had said that to me. It worked then and it would work now. I double-clicked on the torso and closed my eyes slowly. Heather Connelly had been lashed viciously.

I heard my husband walking down the hallway. It sounded like he was headed for the kitchen. He was probably going to get some Dole pineapple out of the refrigerator. It was his habit to eat fruit, especially pineapple, when he woke up. I shut the computer down. Since he had arisen from the dead, I saw no reason not to take advantage of his sculptured physique. In other words, I was going to get some.

# CHAPTER 45

I was naked and spread eagle when Keyth returned. The lights were on and he focused on my crotch. Using a fork, he ate a few pineapple chunks, then took a sip of the juice as he chewed. I could hear him smacking. He walked over to the bed and looked down at me. I smiled.

I said, "Be creative with the juice since you like it so much."

He grinned and sat beside me. Then he put the bowl directly over my erect nipples and let the sweet juice drip on them. I sucked air between my teeth when I felt the cold beverage run from my breasts to my stomach.

"Cold, huh?" Keyth said.

"Uh-huh."

With his moist warm tongue, he lapped at my breasts. The sensation made me shiver. I felt my desire for sex increase significantly. I wanted a quickie. I wanted to do the nasty badly. I wanted to do some reckless, old-fashioned thrusting with my husband. Keyth liked to build on the foreplay. Don't get me wrong, I love foreplay, but at that moment, I didn't need it. I needed immediate penetration.

I pulled Keyth onto the bed and almost yanked down his drawers. His erection stood tall and proud. Normally I would have had to ease down so as not to hurt myself. But not then. I just plopped down on his pole, taking all of him. The fit was snug, like it was made specifically for me. I felt Keyth starting to move with me, but I didn't want that. It was messing up my rhythm.

I said, "Don't move. Just relax. Let me do this."

Keyth put his hands behind his head and watched me pleasure myself. I'm not going to lie. I wasn't thinking about him at all. This was for me. This was what I wanted. This was what I needed. I felt my orgasm building like a campfire, which was threatening to become a four-alarm fire. I moaned and squeezed my nipples, completely oblivious to everything in the room, including my husband. It was just me, his hardness, and my sensitive nipples.

I felt my orgasm release, but it was just a small one, nothing like the one I was going to have. This one was only the prelude to the eruption that was to come. After the initial orgasm, my furious gallop increased in speed and ferocity. I could hear my moans growing in magnitude, in volume, in intensity.

"Savannah gon' wake up, baby," Keyth warned.

I didn't care if I woke up the dead. I was about to explode and that's all that mattered at that point. If we got caught making love by our daughter, we would just have to explain that this was what married adults did and that there was absolutely nothing wrong with it.

I shuddered a little when my orgasm began. Then, as it released itself fully and completely, I screamed like a woman in an Alfred Hitchcock film. My legs felt so weak that it was all I could do to roll off my husband. I was through, but Keyth wasn't. He needed to be taken care of now, but I wasn't in any condition to help him out. He would have to get it on his own. I was done. Finished. Through.

Keyth climbed on top of me, put my limber legs on his shoulders and thrust himself inside me as if he were drilling for oil. Soon, I felt my orgasm building again, which I knew wouldn't take nearly as long as the first. I began moving with my husband. We were one, pulling back, and then thrusting at the exact same time. He was moaning. I was moaning. It was absolutely incredible. I could feel sweat pouring off Keyth's back. It was that intense. And then I came again—powerfully—so did my husband. After we caught our collective breaths, we laughed loudly.

# CHAPTER 46

As I walked Savannah to school, I asked her how she felt about Sarah Lawford's passing. She assured me that she was doing okay. I was skeptical, however. I wondered if that had something to do with her fighting. I had told her she could fight to defend herself and others, but I wondered if it was a reaction to the violent death of a teacher she'd loved who lived right across the street from us.

I had asked both Savannah and the babysitter if they'd seen anything. Neither did. The window of Savannah's bedroom faced Sarah Lawford's house. For all I knew, she could have been looking across the street every night at bedtime, letting frustration and anger fester. And if she was anything like her mother, she had a quick temper, though I'd never seen it. But like they say, "The apple doesn't fall far from the tree."

I met with Anthony George, principal of Henson Academy. He informed me that he had already gotten one of the female teachers to paddle the two girls and Savannah. Mr. George went on to explain that since the girls understood what they had done, a light whack on the rear was all that was necessary. That was because Henson had a strong fast rule that if there's a fight, all the principals get a lick or two. Savannah didn't complain about the paddling and Mr. George had handled the matter, so I left the academy feeling good about the situation.

I walked back home and got into my Mustang. It was my turn to pick Kelly up. We had a rendezvous with the post office on Pennsylvania Avenue, which was only a few blocks from Sterling's hotel.

I called Kelly's cell. I could hear her and what sounded like Sterling laughing. I hoped she was ready. She had been with him since about six-thirty the night before. That should have been enough time to take care of all her needs.

"Hello," Kelly said.

"I'm about a mile away. You ready?" I asked pleasantly.

"Somebody got a little last night, I see," Kelly said.

"I get mine on the regular, Kelly," I said. "And it's still good."

"Normally I would want all the details. But I have details of my own." Kelly laughed.

"Just be downstairs when I pull up. I have some interesting information from a Detective Thompson out in Malibu."

# CHAPTER 47

Kelly McPherson was standing in front of the Willard when I pulled up to the entrance. She opened the door, picked up the faxed copies I had gotten from Detective Thompson, and hopped in. I whipped right back into traffic and proceeded to the post office.

"Any photos?" Kelly asked.

"Yes, but I didn't print them out," I said.

Kelly continued reading. "So the killer was in Malibu, huh? And he raped and killed three women?"

"Apparently," I said. "Skip down to the coroner's conclusion."

Kelly shuffled the papers and began reading the final statements. She looked at me and frowned. "So there are two killers?"

"Either that, or the killer is ambidextrous."

"What are the chances of that, Phoenix?"

"Probably none. We've got two killers," I said.

"But, did you notice that the killer's MO doesn't exactly fit all of ours."

"What do you mean?"

"In Malibu, the walls were splattered with blood from the body parts being thrown against the walls."

"So?"

"So Sarah Lawford's body parts weren't thrown against the wall. Neither were Warden Perkins' nor his wife's. Yet, Taylor Hoffman's body parts were."

"What are you saying, Phoenix?"

"I'm not saying anything. I'm simply articulating the facts as we know them. The killer in Malibu was pissed at his victims and Taylor Hoffman. Drugs were found in Heather Connelly's system. Who knows what we're going to find in Hoffman's system? Those two murders are very similar. Both homes had an abundance of sex toys. Dildos, vaginal lubricants, flavored condoms, et cetera. If the coroner finds cocaine in Hoffman's system, I have to believe that Hoffman and Connelly were connected to Perkins and Blake. The troubling thing is, none of this makes any sense. Hoffman and Connelly were already well-off.

"Yeah, Phoenix. Why even get involved in the drug trade? Assuming they are."

"Greed. People never have enough. They always want more. You oughta see the Connelly mansion,

Kelly. It's absolutely gorgeous. Probably has every imaginable amenity. She had a thirteen-car garage full of expensive automobiles. Her friends were rich, too. They found a friggin' Lamborghini Diablo that belonged to Sandra Rhodes at LAX."

"You know what they say." Kelly laughed. "The rich get richer. Now you know why."

# CHAPTER 48

The line was out the door and it was a blistering day already. The D.C. heat was already at eighty degrees with ninety-percent humidity. I wasn't about to wait in line to see the manager. We clipped our credentials to our belt buckles and walked into the lobby. It was hotter in there than it was outside. The customers were taking off garments and fanning themselves. I could hear the customers grumbling as we walked past everybody and entered the inner lobby. They wanted to know why we didn't get in line like everybody else. I saw five postal clerks behind the counter waiting on customers. One of the clerks was catching hell from a fiery lady of about fifty years.

"What the hell do you mean, you don't have any thirty-seven-cent stamps?" the lady asked.

"I'm sorry, ma'am, but..."

"You damn right, you're sorry!" the lady shouted. "Let me ask you something. If you went to

McDonald's for lunch, stood in a long line, got to the counter and asked for a cheeseburger, and the employee tells you they're out of hamburger meat, what would you say?"

I tried not to laugh. But the biddy had a point. It was ridiculous for the post office to run out of stamps.

"Well, Ma'am, I don't have anything to do with the stamps. That's the manager's job."

"And where the fuck is he?" The lady continued her tirade. "He's never here when you try to register a complaint. He's not here when you call this dump."

"Ma'am, you can fill out a customer complaint card and register your complaint in writing," the clerk said, almost pleading.

"I just don't understand how the hell you can run out of stamps when they're your bread and butter."

The clerk just looked at her without saying a word. The rage in her eyes was on the verge of erupting. I could tell the woman wanted to give the customer a serious tongue-lashing of her own, but there was nothing she could do. She had to take it and try to be pleasant.

"That'll be fifty-nine dollars and forty-five cents, Ma'am," the clerk said.

The lady opened her purse to get the money. "I've forgotten my money," she said. "You do accept American Express, I presume?"

"Yes. We accept all major credit cards."

The lady handed the clerk the card and she slid it through the credit card machine. Apparently, nothing happened. She slid it through five more times.

"Ma'am, this card isn't registering for some reason. Do you have another card?"

"JESUS CHRIST!" the woman yelled and wiped sweat from her forehead. "First you don't have stamps. Now your fucking machine won't work." She handed the clerk another card. "If that one doesn't work, I'll just write a check. And don't you dare tell me you don't accept checks. I'll fucking lose my mind!"

The clerk slid the card through the machine and looked at the woman. "I guess the system's down, Ma'am."

"YOU GUESS! Forget it. Give me the packages back. I'll go to the post office on Virginia Avenue. I bet their air conditioning is working. And I bet they have stamps."

"Ma'am I can't give you back all of your mail. Your express mail just left on a dispatch. You have to pay for this before you leave."

"Let me get this straight. You don't have stamps. Your credit card machine doesn't work, but you can get a dispatch out on time?" The woman shook her head, then wrote out a check and stormed out in a huff.

# CHAPTER 49

I showed my credentials and said, "FBI. I'm Special Agent Perry and this is Agent McPherson. I need to see someone about a post office box." I could see the fear in the clerk's eyes, which is typical when we introduce ourselves. It's kind of like being in traffic. When you see a police car, the first thing you do is check your speed. You want to make sure you're not speeding.

The clerk put up a closed sign and told us to meet her at the door in the outer lobby where the post office boxes were located. I'm sure she was glad to get away from customers for a while. A few seconds passed and the clerk let us in. Her nameplate read: Geraldine. No last name.

"Hi, Geraldine," I said. "We need to look through your computer to run a trace on the users of Box 12666."

"Sure, but we don't have computer systems for PO boxes."

Kelly and I looked at each other. I was starting to understand how the angry woman who had just left felt. These people were still writing things down, which meant we would have to rely on them to be able to find what we're looking for. From what I'd seen so far, if they didn't have stamps, they probably didn't have a good system for post box rentals.

"Well, how do you keep track of who uses your boxes?" Kelly asked.

"We use form 1091A. We write their names and addresses on cards like these." She handed me one.

"Who's renting Box 12666?" I asked.

"Let me see," Geraldine said and began sifting through the cards. "This might take a few minutes. They're separated by the due date. We rent them six months or a year at a time."

"We just need a name and an address, if you have it," I said politely. "Then we'll be out of your hair."

"Ah, here it is," she said. "Dwight Rappaport. 656 Kingsbridge Drive in Alexandria."

"Do you have a phone number?" Kelly asked.

"No. We don't require that sort of information," she said. "What's this all about? Is this about those rash of murders we've been hearing about?"

"That's classified," I said, politely. Geraldine looked disappointed. "Who had the box before Mr. Rappaport?"

"There's no way of knowing that. We don't keep the records on file. Once you give the box up and another renter takes it over, we throw away the information on the previous renter."

"How long has Mr. Rappaport had this box?" Kelly asked.

"All that information is on the card. I'll make a copy for you."

"Thanks. You've been a big help."

# CHAPTER 50

Dwight Rappaport could be the killer, I thought. On the other hand, he may not be. According to the copy of the 1091A form that Geraldine gave us, the PO box was being used for business. He'd had the box for seven years. Rappaport Specialties was the name he used. I wondered how much revenue he was pulling in, so I called the library on my cell and had the librarian do a little research while we drove to Alexandria.

According to the librarian, there wasn't much information on Rappaport Specialties. The Directorate of Corporate Affiliations states that Rappaport Specialties had been a viable business for seven years. Annual revenues exceeded one and a half-million dollars. The business had no employees, which told me he probably had an Internet business and worked out of his home. If so, he might be there when we arrived.

If he wasn't the killer, he still would have to explain why he ordered the bullwhips. And if he sold them, he would at least have records—maybe even addresses. The case was finally starting to break. This was going to be good. I could feel it.

I parked the Mustang in front of Rappaport's house. His home looked like it could be on the cover of a magazine. In fact, all the homes on his block could have. If Rappaport was the killer, I wondered how much of a shock it would be for his neighbors.

When we got out of the car, we could hear the faint sound of classical music coming from inside his house. As we approached the front door, the music became louder and louder. I recognized the tune. It was Hans Zimmer's "Vide Cor Meum" from the *Hannibal* soundtrack.

I rang the doorbell and waited. I rang again. I knocked. I beat on the door. Finally, I tried opening the door, but it was locked. We walked around the house, looking through windows for any sign of life. From what I could tell, the house was well-furnished and decorated, but I didn't see anyone.

We continued further along the side of the house. A curtain was partially open and we saw a man sitting in a chair completely naked, watching a videotape of a woman in bondage. He was masturbating with his left hand while holding a .45-caliber pistol to his head with his right hand. The hammer was cocked and ready to fire. He could blow his brains out at any moment.

Kelly and I had disgusted looks on our faces as we watched the man play a foolish game of Russian Roulette as he pleasured himself. Through the mirror that hung on the wall above the television, we could see that he was on the verge of climaxing. His face contorted more and more as his back and forth motion increased. His mouth and eyes opened as his seed spurted.

Just then, at that critical moment, as his scions splashed against the television screen, he saw us watching him. Out of pure fright, he jerked and the gun went off. Gray matter rocketed across the room and stained the wall crimson.

I was completely flabbergasted. My mouth was open. My eyes bulged. Kelly, too. I could see our image in the mirror. The morbid part about seeing the man blow his brains out was that I was thinking, if he was Dwight Rappaport, he was probably our best chance at wrapping the case up,

# CHAPTER 51

I kicked in the back door and we blew into the house like a hurricane, weapons drawn. For all we knew, there could be others in the house. Who knew, maybe a sexual orgy was going on. Detective Thompson had drawn that conclusion in Malibu. And if there were others, they could be the killers. We found the room where the fresh stiff was, but finished clearing the house. "Vide Cor Meum" was still blasting throughout the house. It stopped playing for a second or two, then began again.

After securing the house, we went back to the room where our suspect was still sitting in a fixed position, looking like someone had scared him, still holding the gun. Kelly went to a quieter room and called headquarters. I looked at the fresh cadaver. His pubic hair had been shaved and his penis was abnormally large. The man was still hard. This was one for the annals.

I stood in front of the man, trying not to step in any of the semen that still oozed from his phallus. His hand had locked onto his genitals. With the music as loud as it was, I couldn't hear what was going on in the video, so I looked for the stereo. It was across the room. I noticed a Sansui remote on the desk next to a handwritten note I presumed was written by the dead man, explaining why he had killed himself in this fashion.

After putting on a pair of surgical gloves, I picked up the remote and silenced the house from the cacophony coming from the other side of the room. Immediately I heard the sound of flesh being whipped. I turned around and looked at what was happening in the video. A woman was hanging upside-down in anti-gravity boots while she was being beaten. Unlike the women in Malibu and the women in D.C., the woman in the video wasn't bleeding.

Moments later the tape ran out and no one had gotten killed. I hit the eject button. The video was titled *Sugar & Spice*. It was a strange title, but I didn't think much of it. I put the video back in. We had hit the jackpot. No matter who this guy was, the fact that he was watching the video in the house of the guy we were looking for had convinced me that this was our guy. And if this man wasn't Dwight Rappaport, maybe Rappaport was the other man.

For some reason, I noticed that the woman's genitals in the video were shaved, too. Why? Was this some sort of mimicking ritual? I looked at the note again. I reached for it.

*To whom it may concern:*

*If you have this letter, I am dead. I wrote it to let you know that I wasn't trying to kill myself. I was attempting to heighten my sexual pleasure by adding an element of danger that would certainly lead to my death if the gun went off, which it apparently has. Why real bullets, you ask? Because without an actual threat, without the real chance of the gun going off, I would not receive any fulfillment. Believe me; I tried using blanks on more than one occasion.*

*Now that you know what I was doing and why, please be decent enough to keep what happened to me from my parents. They are great people with high moral standards. The idea of knowing that their only son had died in such a manner would haunt them for the rest of their natural lives. They would be blamed for my experimentation and it had nothing to do with them. My own sexual deviance led me to an early grave.*

It was signed Dwight Rappaport.

"Kelly," I said when I heard her come back into the room. "What'll you bet this guy is from California?"

"Probably," Kelly said.

I looked at Rappaport. He was bald. I frowned when I noticed that he didn't have any facial hair at all. No eyebrows. No eyelashes. He hadn't shaved his genitals; the hair had fallen out, I realized. Rappaport may have had alopecia universalis, a skin disease responsible for the loss of all bodily hair. Some people are born with it.

Rappaport had to be the killer. Or at least one of them, I thought. All the evidence pointed to him, yet, in my bones, in my heart, I knew it was just too neat. We were lucky to find out that the whips had come from the land down under and that bit of information led us to Rappaport, who conveniently blew his brains out right in front of us.

I think I would have felt better if we had found him dead. That way, I could at least think someone killed him to shut him up. But being a witness to self-annihilation blows away that theory. *Damn!* Why did we have to hear that music and go in search of a way in? If we had maybe come a few minutes later, he would have been finished and we could have at least questioned him. We could have learned or confirmed a few things.

# CHAPTER 52

We searched Rappaport's house, hoping to find something, anything that would link him to the murders. Sure, we had the videotape he was watching, but any first-year Georgetown law student could get that thrown out if that's all we had. A lawyer might argue that his taste in videos doesn't prove he murdered anyone, which is true.

Unless we found the whips and forensics could prove that the whips were the same ones used in Malibu and D.C., we were at a dead end again. Dwight Rappaport was innocent until we proved he did the murders. And the only way we were going to do that was by finding the other killer. As far as I was concerned, one of the vicious killers was off the streets. Unfortunately, the other man was still at large, and we had to wait until he killed again so that we could collect more clues.

"Phoenix, look at this," Kelly said from inside the closet.

I walked over and looked in. There was a replica of Rappaport's penis hanging on a coat hook. *The Plow* was stenciled on it. "I've heard of porn stars having their organs molded for a fee and a percentage," I said.

Apparently Dwight Rappaport had made his fortune from the royalties he earned by allowing an artificial penis manufacturer to mold his abnormally large organ.

According to Rappaport's ledgers, he was marketing sex toys. Evidently there is a huge market for edible lingerie, handcuffs, whips, paddles, blindfolds, butt plugs, lubricants, vibrators, flavored condoms, et cetera. We had found invoices and a ledger full of filled orders. No names and addresses, just stock numbers, dates, and prices. From our search, we knew that he didn't keep his merchandise in his home, which meant he probably hired a shipping and receiving company to handle the orders while he raked in the cash.

I flipped open my cell and called Season Chambers. She had offered to help us in any way she could. Season had told me she wanted to get the killer of innocent women off the streets. I thought that if I offered her the exclusive, she would honor Rappaport's wishes. I think the man was a creep, but he had a point. The media would be all over this if his cause of death was reported. I personally don't care for nor do I trust the media. But Season was woman enough to apologize to my face and offer her services. Giving Season the chance to read the note and actually get a look at the crime scene could be the beginning of building a good relationship with her.

Inside of an hour, Rappaport's home was crawling with FBI agents. They were going through everything, even the trash. As I spoke with Season Chambers, I could hear the constant chatter of the forensics team. They talked about dinner and joked about the firm grip Rappaport had on his tool, the drying semen on the television screen, and gray matter on the wall.

"You ever see a stiff with a GSW to the head?" I asked her. Season frowned. She really was green. "A gunshot wound," I explained.

"No," she said, her eyes filled with fright.

I said, "Prepare yourself. I couldn't tell you on the cell, but the man is naked and he was masturbating with a gun to his head. The gun went off. Now you have your first exclusive. Don't make it your last. Keep what I show you in confidence, agreed?"

"Agreed."

Season Chambers wasn't in the room five seconds before she doubled over, put both hands over her mouth, and ran.

# CHAPTER 53

The coroner found traces of cocaine in Taylor Hoffman's system. It was looking more and more like a drug connection at Norrell Prison. I wondered if Jack Hoffman was somehow running drugs out to California on his many jaunts to the West Coast. He was back in town and Kelly and I were on our way to talk to him. The good news, if you could call it that, was the coroner thought two men had killed both Sarah Lawford and Taylor Hoffman. If Dwight Rappaport was one of the men, we still had one on the loose.

Kortney Malone, our illustrious acting director, against my wishes, decided to have a press conference. She announced that we had tracked one of the killers "who had committed suicide while performing a sexual act on himself," was how she put it. I had told her not to do it, but Kortney thought it would help smoke out the other killer. She went on to say how sexually depraved these men were and how we were closing in. We weren't even close to closing in, I'd told her. If the other man decided to stop the killings on his own, he'd get away scot-free.

"You see why I don't like Kortney, Phoenix?" Kelly said.

I laughed. "Yeah. But let's give her a chance. We women have to stick together."

"Sticking together may ultimately lead to our own demise." Kelly laughed. "But I'll give her a chance."

I parked the Mustang in front of the Hoffman house and we got out of the car. "Phoenix, this could be a big waste of time. You know that, don't you?"

"Yeah, I know. But we gotta follow every lead. You know that, right?"

"Yep," she said in a ho-hum way.

I rang the doorbell. "Jack Hoffman?" I said when a man opened the door.

"Yes," he said.

"I'm Special Agent Perry, and this is Agent McPherson. I know this is a bad time, sir. But we need to ask you a few questions."

# CHAPTER 54

J ack Hoffman confirmed our suspicions. He and Taylor did use cocaine that night but they were not involved in trafficking. He told us that they had celebrated that night by going out for an expensive dinner. When they returned, they both did a couple of lines and made love. They showered and Taylor took him to Dulles. We believed him, which meant we had come to another dead end.

"You ready to call it a night, Phoenix?"

"Yes, but we're not going to," I said. "We're going back to the lab and opening Rappaport's hard drive. We might find something there. I know it's been a long disappointing day, but I want to see what's there."

We hadn't found anything connecting Dwight Rappaport to drugs or to the killings. All we had was his address and the fact that his postal box received three bullwhips. There was something to that. I knew it.

I opened the hard drive and did some snooping. It occurred to me that Si Davey had been contacted via the Internet. Since Dwight Rappaport had ordered the whips online, and given his penchant for sexual bondage, there was a chance that the other man may be into the same things. If so, perhaps they kept in contact through email. That's what I was really looking for. Someone he may have met in a chat room.

Lucky for us, Rappaport had kept a lot of his email. However, there was so much of it, it was going to take some time to track down all of the names and addresses. We started by disregarding all mail that came in after the Perkins murders. If Rappaport were one of the men we were looking for, he would have had the partner earlier. We concentrated on the previous email.

There were letters about the products he sold, but most were asking about bondage, offering to play sex games with him. I was thinking, there are some really sick people out there—lots of them. It occurred to me that most of the people were writing one letter so we eliminated them for the time being and concentrated on those he corresponded with at least three times. I wanted to know who these degenerates were and where they lived.

We had narrowed the search down to about two

hundred screen names. It was time to call it a night. We were going to let the computer techs do their thing. By morning, we would have another lead. Problem was the other killer may not have been among the list of names we'd given the techs. And even if he was, he may not live in the D.C. area. But it was all we had, so we had to roll with it.

# CHAPTER 55

Season Chambers had just finished broadcasting the eleven o'clock news and was on her way home. It had been a long day. Seeing Dwight Rappaport sitting in his den with his hand locked onto his privates and his brains splattered against the wall had been a vivid memory that had resurfaced all day. She was glad to be going home, but she wished she didn't have to be home alone. Season Chambers was a driven twenty-four-year-old woman who had made up her mind to become an anchorwoman at a network.

The fact that Phoenix Perry had selected her for the exclusive story on the chain saw murders was evidence that she was well on her way. After all, Phoenix was an FBI agent. Season believed that this was just the beginning. The bureau would eventually catch the other maniac and another would rear his ugly head. Then another and another. And with any luck, if she kept her word to Phoenix, she would become a liaison of sorts with a pipeline inside the bureau. If only I had met Phoenix when the assassin was in town a couple of months ago, she thought.

Season Chambers felt her stomach growl. She hadn't eaten all day. Who could blame her after seeing Dwight Rappaport's brains all over the wall and his scions on the television screen. She shook her head slowly as she relived what she had seen for the hundredth time that day. She pulled into Wendy's and ordered a grilled chicken salad with a Diet Coke.

Twenty minutes later, she pulled into her garage and went into the house. She hung her keys on the rack just inside the house. "I'm so glad to be home," she said aloud.

"We're glad you're home, too, Season," Terry said. "After all, it is your turn."

# CHAPTER 56

The waiting game was difficult for me. I had hoped to get something from the techs early in the day, but so far, I hadn't heard a thing. We were close to breaking the case wide open. Coco Nimburu had once told me that the clues were right in front of me. I was missing something. But what? I knew it was something we were taking for granted. It could be the smallest, most insignificant thing. It was probably something that we wouldn't even consider. Later, Kelly and I would go back over everything we had. Together, maybe we could figure it out.

I had taken Savannah to the library earlier and I had the strangest feeling we were being watched. I found myself turning around several times to see who it was that found my daughter and me so interesting. I had assumed it was a man checking me out, but I never saw anyone looking in our direction. But the feeling persisted until we left.

On the way home, we stopped by Blockbuster Video and picked up a copy of *The Hurricane* for me and Keyth. Savannah wanted to see *Star Wars: The Phantom Menace*. I made spaghetti and meatballs for dinner and put a loaf of buttered garlic bread in the oven. It was good to have a normal day in my fast-paced life.

After we finished eating, Savannah went into our room and watched her movie while Keyth and I watched *The Hurricane* in the family room. We were halfway into the picture when the phone rang.

"Hello," I said.

"We got an address, Agent Perry," the tech said.

"What took so long?" I asked.

"One of the techs found it at about three a.m.," the tech said. "He told me to tell you at a decent hour this morning, but I forgot."

I was pissed, but I didn't let on. I wanted to say that another woman might be dead because you forgot. Instead, I said, "What's the address?"

"It's one of the prisoners at Norrell. They were using a library computer."

A broad smile flashed across my face. This was it. The break we were waiting for. Then I frowned. I said, "How can a prisoner be involved? He may have access to the Internet, but that's as far as it goes."

"I don't know, Agent Perry. But I do apologize for not passing this vital information on earlier."

"No problem," I said and hung up the phone. I picked up the remote and paused the film. "Keyth, does it make sense to you that a prisoner at Norrell is committing the crimes?"

"Yes. Given what's been going on out there. Hell yeah! They probably let the prisoners out at night. Who knows?"

"Maybe it wasn't a prisoner at all. Salaam Khan may have been right all along. It may have been Captain Callahan. He would have just as much access to the computers as prisoners. More, in fact. Trouble is, he's already up on charges. Why would he do this? I can perhaps understand the warden. Money may have been the issue there. But what about the rest? Could Callahan have flown out to Malibu to do the Connelly mansion murders, then flown back?"

"Good questions. Every one of them. You and Kelly better get back out to the prison and ask some questions. And be ready for anything. If you're right, if it is Callahan, you'd better take an army of agents with you. They've got an arsenal at that prison."

# CHAPTER 57

"She's gotta go!" Terry said, and continued cleaning a rifle. "You know the rules. It's her turn!"

"No!" Jerry said. "If we kill an FBI agent, we'll bring all kinds of heat on ourselves. We can't afford that. Not right now."

"Sooner or later, we're going to have to deal with her," Terry said, and started reassembling the rifle.

Jerry said, "Rather than kill her, let's discourage her. Or better yet, let's hire some guys to put her outta commission."

"Yeah, but who, Jerry?" Terry asked while aiming the silenced rifle at a red and white target over a hundred yards away. "Alex says she's Bruce Lee reincarnated. Whoever we get had better be good."

Jerry, looking at the target through binoculars, said, "We'd better be there just in case. If it goes the other way, and she captures them, they might tell her who sent them."

Terry squeezed off five rounds, all of them dead center. "Eventually there's going to be a showdown. You know that, don't you? And I'm not going back to prison."

"I know, Terry."

"So when do you wanna do this?"

"After tonight, we cool it. Let's see what they come up with. Eventually they'll relax and that's when we'll take her out of the picture. Kelly McPherson, too. But first we gotta get Phoenix."

# CHAPTER 58

I led twenty agents into Norrell prison. Captain Callahan was shocked to see us back, but he didn't resist. When I told him why we were there, he laughed hysterically. I got the feeling that I was barking up the wrong tree. But this was where the emails originated. There was no doubt about that. If Captain Callahan wasn't involved, someone at the prison was. It could have been anybody.

"Do you have a furlough program here, Captain?" I asked.

"No."

"Are you allowing special privileges?"

"Special privileges?" he repeated with a questioning tone.

"Are you allowing any of the trustees to leave the prison at night for any reason?" I asked.

Captain Callahan doubled over with laughter. "You brought a battalion of men here and you don't even know who you're looking for? I got news for you, Missy; I didn't have anything to do with the warden's murder, and no one here did. Look around all you like. Talk to whomever you want. You don't have nothin' on me, my officers, or on any of my prisoners."

He was right. We didn't have much, but we were desperate. The strange thing was, I believed him. I got the feeling that the only thing that Captain Callahan was guilty of was running drugs out of the prison. The sad part was, he might even get off for that. Only one guard was talking. And he was the accuser. No one was corroborating his story. The guards had even gotten rid of the drugs. D.C. Metro didn't have much of a case against him.

"Maybe you didn't. Maybe you did. Where's the library? I wanna see all the computers. Somebody at this prison knows something and I'm not leaving until we find out who it is."

The truth was we could have been intentionally led here. Everybody knew about the warden's murder. The real killer could have led us here to throw us off his trail, but we had to check the computers out anyway. Captain Callahan could have been lying, but I really didn't think he was. It was frustrating as hell.

We swarmed into the computer lab like a bunch of locusts. One by one, each agent turned on a computer and began examining it. I'm all for educating prisoners, but I questioned the wisdom of allowing prisoners access to the Internet and allowing email addresses. That, to me, was trouble waiting to happen.

After several hours of fruitless searching, I asked, "Are there any more computers?"

"There are a couple in the warden's office," Captain Callahan said. He was quite calm, showing no evidence of anything to hide. Then, as though it was an afterthought, he said, "The women have computers in their prison, too, if you wanna look."

"Do you and your officers have access to the women's prison?"

"Yes."

"Then I wanna see them," I said.

Kelly assigned a couple of our guys to the warden's office. Then we went to the women's prison.

# CHAPTER 59

One of the guards had used a computer in the women's prison so as not to draw suspicion on himself, I thought as we walked through the cages, where women yelled out all kinds of obscenities at us.

"Five minutes is all I need with you, darlin'," one said.

Another said, "I'm all the woman you need, little girl. Come on in here and let Mabel teach you somethin' 'bout yo'self."

"Y'all can have little stuff. Gimme the blond," another said and flicked her tongue in and out like a snake.

"Here, Blondie," another inmate said, pulling her fingers out of her vagina and offering them to Kelly. "My kitty cat tastes good. Wanna taste?" When Kelly ignored her, she put her fingers in her mouth. "Umm! Umm! Good. Just like Campbell Soup."

"Is the library open, Captain Callahan?" I asked, ignoring the catcalls by depraved, incarcerated women.

"Surely there was another way to get there, Captain," Kelly said.

"Yeah, but I woulda deprived the girls of their fun." He laughed. "And just to show what a nice guy I am, McPherson, I'll let you have your choice of any one of them." He laughed again.

Kelly frowned. "That's disgusting."

"Some of these women have been locked up for twenty years. What do you expect? Girl Scouts?"

"And you let these women prey on each other?" Kelly asked.

"Survival of the fittest. We can't watch 'em twenty-four hours a day. Besides, all of them were convicted. They weren't kidnapped. They get what they get."

Kelly shook her head and mumbled something. A few minutes later, we were out of general population and entering the prison library. I saw a young black woman behind the counter reading *A Raisin in the Sun*. She looked like she belonged in a library that didn't have bars. I wondered how old she was and what was her crime. She didn't fit. The other women looked and acted like they belonged behind bars, but not this woman. Had someone molested this delicate-looking woman? I wondered how long it would be before she turned into an animal, too.

I showed the woman my credentials. I'm not sure why. I guess I wanted to show her a measure of respect. "FBI, Ma'am. We need to go through all of the computers."

"May I ask why?" the young woman asked.

May I? She was educated, I thought. How did an educated black woman end up at Norrell? I stared at her for a few seconds, wondering what the difference was between us.

"Agent Perry," she said politely, snapping me out of it.

"Uh, yeah. I'm sorry. Someone may have been using these computers to communicate with a suspected murderer."

The other agents, including Kelly, fanned out, turning on computers. I stood there at the counter, thinking, if her daddy had been like mine, maybe she wouldn't be here.

"May I ask you a question, young lady?"

"Aggravated murder," she said without hesitation. Her soft eyes hardened as if she was reliving the murder. "I killed the man who stripped me of my dignity. The jury let him off. I was the one he raped and that was good enough for me."

"Where'd you go to school?"

"Howard University," she said.

"That's my alma mater," I said. "What's your name?"

"Dawn McNeil," she answered and extended her hand. "Sorry to meet you under these circumstances."

"I'm sorry, too," I said. "Did you finish school?"

"Actually no, I didn't. Well, yes. I completed my bachelor's and I was working on my master's when I was raped. I had studied criminology and had planned on becoming an FBI agent." She shook her head. "Life sure is funny, isn't it? Here you are doing what I wanted to do. I was supposed to be arresting criminals and I ended up being one."

She kinda laughed sardonically. I didn't see any humor in it. Sarcastic or otherwise. In fact, I felt a profound sadness when I looked at her in her prison dungarees.

"When are you getting out?"

"I have about six months left on a two-year stretch."

"That's good. You'll be out soon."

"Yes, the judge cut me a lot of slack, given my reasons for killing the bastard. But what do I have to look forward to? My life is over. I'm a felon."

"You still interested in fighting crime?"

"Yes, but there's no way that's going to happen now."

"It might. I'm the majority owner in my husband's private investigation firm. Have you been working on your master's while you've been in?"

"No, I didn't see much point to it."

"I'll tell you what, finish your master's, or at least work on it until you get out, and I'll set you up with a job," I said. "So how long have you been working in the library, Dawn?"

"Since July fifth. The woman who was running the library at the time thought I'd make a good librarian since I came in every day to read."

"Where is she now?"

"I don't know. She got out and I haven't heard from her since. Smart girl. Rich, too. At least that's what she told me. She said she had a house out in Malibu."

"What?" My heart thumped hard and fast. "Kelly, come and listen to this."

Kelly came over. "No luck so far, Phoenix. I'm afraid this is another wild goose chase."

"No. Dawn was telling me about the woman who was the librarian before her. She claimed to be rich and guess where she was from?" Kelly frowned. "Malibu."

"What?" Kelly beamed.

"What was her name, Dawn?" I asked.

"Never knew her first name. Last name was Connelly though."

"Agent Perry, we found it," one of the agents said.

# CHAPTER 60

Connelly's records were missing. There were no hard copies and the computer records had been erased. According to Captain Callahan, her lawyer had argued that she entered the system as a juvenile and the only reason she had her sentence lengthened was because she had tried to escape, which landed her in Norrell. Therefore, she was a first-class citizen with the same rights and privileges as everybody else. She could even vote.

"What do you make of all of this, Kelly?" I asked.

"I think we're lucky as hell. That's what I think. But luck aside, we don't know jack! So what? A Connelly was in prison here and a Connelly was murdered in Malibu. Maybe they were sisters. Maybe they were the same person. Who knows? The bottom line is, there's still a guy out there killing women—viciously I might add. This is one big mess. We keep running around from place to place and keep coming up short. What little bit of information we get leads right back where we started."

"Maybe that's the key, Kelly. Maybe we need to start all over. Go back to the beginning and figure this out."

"Dawn, what was Connelly in for?"

"Same as me. Aggravated murder. But she was a juvenile when she did the deed and her million-dollar lawyer got it plea-bargained down to man-slaughter. Don't get me wrong, I liked Connelly. She helped me get this cushy job here in the library. But get this, the word is, she killed her mother because her mother threatened to expose her father for incest if he didn't give her what she wanted in the divorce settlement."

I frowned. "I don't mean to sound morbid, but why was she protecting her father? He was the one having sex with his own daughter."

Dawn laughed. "That's the strange thing, Agent Perry. She told me that she and her father were in love."

"Kelly," I said, "What'll you bet these folks are from California?"

Kelly laughed. "Where's the father now?"

"Killed himself a couple of years ago," Dawn said.

"Was he jackin' off?" I asked.

Kelly laughed.

"I don't get it," Dawn said frowning.

My cell rang. "Agent Perry."

"Kortney Malone here. Get over to Season Chambers' house. She's been killed."

# CHAPTER 61

Why Season Chambers? I thought as we walked into the midst of onlookers who didn't seem to mind the ninety-seven-degree temperature. What was the pattern? There had to be one. All these nuts had one. We had to find it. Maybe Season figured something out and the killer had to shut her up. We had to find out who the other killer was and fast. Eleven people were dead and the killings were still mounting.

We walked into Season Chambers' house. The crime lab team was already there collecting what little evidence the killer left. I knew what they'd find. It would be the same as all the others. But still, I needed to see the crime scene for myself. We still hadn't figured out why some of the women's body parts were thrown against the wall and why others weren't. All we knew or rather believed was that the killer was angry with some and not angry with others, which made no sense.

Kelly and I went up to Season Chambers' bedroom. The air conditioning kept the body parts cool. It would be difficult to pinpoint an exact time of death—not that it mattered. I looked down into the blue eyes that stared back at me and shook my head. In the near distance, the photographer snapped off photo after photo. The look on Season Chambers' face was one of painful anguish and horrible fear combined. I was thinking, this young woman had just seen her very first crime scene stiff a day earlier. And now she was dead, too. Again I questioned, why this woman? Surely she wasn't involved with drugs.

"Let's search the house, Kelly," I said. "Maybe she found something and didn't have a chance to tell us about it."

"Where do you wanna start, Phoenix?" Kelly asked with resignation. I could tell she was getting tired of the case also.

"The computer. Where else?" I said, knowing we wouldn't find one single solitary clue. But it had to be done. It was procedure. "How long has she been dead?" I asked the coroner just before we left the room.

"About seventeen hours, I'd say," the coroner said.

I looked at my watch. It was six p.m. If the coroner was right, that would mean that she was killed sometime after she finished the nightly broadcast. Kelly and I donned surgical gloves and went into the room where she'd kept her computer.

I said, "You think someone followed her home from work last night?"

"That's what it looks like to me."

"How are they getting in?"

Kelly interrupted a couple of D.C. cops laughing in the hallway. "Guys, was the alarm turned off on this one, too?"

"She didn't have an alarm!" an officer yelled back.

Kelly looked at me and shrugged her shoulders. I shook my head. It amazed me how callous we've become. There was a cut-up young woman not far from where the officers told jokes and laughed. But they weren't bothered at all. Truth be told, if I didn't know Season Chambers, their laughing and joking wouldn't have bothered me. I've done the same thing. It's different when you know the victim.

After an hour of searching, we found exactly what we expected—nothing. I removed my cell from its holder and called home. I wanted to let my family know I wasn't going to make dinner. Keyth answered.

"Hi, sweetheart," I said.

"Hi, yourself."

"I won't be home for dinner tonight. I'm sorry."

"I figured as much. I saw the six o'clock news. Season Chambers wasn't involved with the prison, right?"

"I don't believe so. No."

"Do you guys have anything yet?"

"Not really. Just bits and pieces. Nothing concrete yet. We need a motive. And I'm starting to believe that the warden's murder didn't have anything to do with drugs. Anyway, I'll see you when I get home. Bye."

Next, I called Detective Thompson. I asked him about the Connelly victim. He told me her name was Heather and that she had married John Connelly a few years ago. When I asked him about the daughter, he said that John and his first wife, Caroline, had filed for divorce. She'd moved to Washington and taken the daughter with her.

"What was her name?"

"Alexis Connelly. She's doing time for manslaughter in your neck of the woods."

"No. She was released in early July," I told him. "Has anyone claimed the Malibu property?"

"Not to my knowledge, no."

"Hmmmm. This is way out there. But do you think Alexis Connelly could have hired someone to kill her stepmother?"

"I suppose it's possible, but I doubt it, Agent Perry.

They were the best of friends in high school."

"What!" I said, suddenly frowning. "Her father married her best friend?"

"Yep."

"Fax me the backgrounds on the murdered women. There may be something there, Detective."

# CHAPTER 62

The killings ceased. Two weeks had passed and we hadn't had any new victims that fit the profile of the Lasher. That's what we called him. We had no leads on the other man, if indeed there was another man. Several agents were saying the killings were over because our handwriting expert believed that Rappaport was ambidextrous.

He based his theory on the fact that Dwight Rappaport was masturbating with his left hand. McGregor believed that was his dominate hand and that's why he was using it to pleasure himself. From his suicide note, and the entries in his ledger, our handwriting expert concluded that Rappaport wrote with his right hand. Personally, I think Kortney Malone wanted to wrap up the case so that the bureau would look good—look efficient under her regime.

I thought there was a killer still out there, still

choosing victims by some strange formula. It was just a matter of time before the killer resurfaced.

In the meantime, I was on my way to the dojo. Kelly was supposed to meet me there. She had a lot of time on her hands since Sterling Wise left. She reminded me that I had promised to train with her when I called her from Universal City. Now was as good a time as any. Nothing was happening with the Lasher.

I parked the Mustang, picked up a bag that had my tools, and the sword that Coco Nimburu had given me. I was going to hang the sword. This would be the first time that I'd even been to my dojo since my students were killed a couple of months earlier. It felt strange. I guess I had been avoiding the place. Lots of memories.

I flipped the light switch upwards and illuminated the dojo. I had already decided I was going to hang the sword right under the life-sized photo of a scene from *Enter the Dragon*. There were several scenes from that film and others in the dojo. Most were of Bruce Lee in the basement of the castle fighting Hahn's men. The life-sized one, however, was of Bruce Lee and Bob Wall in their epic showdown on the castle grounds.

I walked over to the stereo and turned it on. Seconds later, I heard Diana Ross and the Supremes' classic hit "I Hear a Symphony." I liked listening to Motown when I worked out. My father practically weaned me on the Motown sound while we were in China. I grew to love it as much as he did. They had such great singers and songwriters during their heyday. Smoky Robinson and the Miracles, the Temptations, the Four Tops, Stevie Wonder, and the Jackson Five. Too bad Berry Gordy had to sell, I thought.

I hung the sword and began my workout. Kelly wasn't going to show for another hour or so. I began with some stretches to warm up my muscles. As I felt my body starting to warm up, I took off my uniform jacket. Underneath I was wearing a black sleeveless shirt with black and white yin and yang symbols on it.

After that, I put on some gloves and went over to the speed bag. I hit it until I felt myself starting to perspire. Next, I skipped rope for about twenty minutes to "Cloud Nine," "What's Goin' On," "Fingertips," and "Psychedelic Shack." By the time I finished, I had a good sweat going. It was time for the real workout—the wooden dummy.

The wooden dummy helped perfect timing, and striking distance. It also improved endurance and trapping techniques. As I struck the wooden dummy, I found myself thinking about my former students: Earl Johns, Valerie Ryan, Greg Fisher, and Karen Monroe. They had all been killed in this very room. That was another reason I hadn't been back. I didn't want to deal with their passing. As long as I didn't come to the dojo, they were still very much alive—even if it was only in my mind.

An hour had passed and I was sitting cross-legged with my eyes closed in front of the sword that I'd hung underneath the Bruce Lee mural. I could smell the fragrance of a mixture of musk and jasmine incense that I'd lit. "Memories" by the Temptations was playing. As I sank deeper and deeper into my mind, the music became distant, but I was cognizant of it and everything around me.

Like flashes of light, pieces of the evidence that we had collected and the dead women came to my mind out of sequence. One second I'd see Sarah Lawford. The next I'd see melted ice cream in her kitchen. I could see Dwight Rappaport sitting in his chair masturbating, then hearing the sound of a bullet discharging and blowing his brains out. I could see the blood-splattered walls in Taylor Hoffman's bedroom. The look on Bernard Rogers' face when he came to Sarah Lawford's home. The picture of Alexis Connelly that Detective Thompson sent me came to mind. She seemed so familiar, but I couldn't place her anywhere. Then there were the receipts. That was the one piece of evidence that we had all overlooked. They all had receipts from the same place.

Suddenly, I felt a presence in my dojo and it wasn't Kelly. This was a hostile presence. Now there were three more. Four altogether.

# CHAPTER 63

I focused on all four men. As they came closer to me, I felt my fear attempt to assert itself. Control and relaxation were the weapons of a true martial artist. If you can control your fear and anger, it's possible to overcome any foe. I inhaled a deep satisfying amount of oxygen and exhaled slowly. I could hear "Dancin' in the Street" playing now.

"The school is closed, gentlemen," I said, still sitting cross-legged and facing the mural.

"We're here to see to it that it stays that way," the man on my right said.

I stood to my feet, my back still facing them. I inhaled deeply again, relaxing every part of my body, preparing for combat. I was ready for anything. I didn't have to see them to know where they were. When I studied under Master Lo, we often used blindfolds, which heightened one's senses. Once I mastered the art, I no longer needed the blindfold to feel antagonism in the air.

With my back still to them, I said, "Is this going to be a fair fight, gentlemen? Or do I have to kick everybody's ass at the same time?"

"We drew straws to see who gets the first crack at the twenty-thousand-dollar bonus," the man to my right said. "And I won."

I smiled. "So, you're here to kill me?" I turned around slowly and faced them. They were all rugged-looking men. Barroom brawlers, every one. The man who had done all of the talking so far looked Spanish. He had dark skin and long black hair, which he wore in a ponytail. They all looked like refugees from a rodeo.

"Not kill, little lady," said the one wearing a black cowboy hat and a black leather vest, no shirt, which showed off his powerfully built arms. He and two others had whips in their hands. "Five-thousand dollars a limb." He went on.

"Let me ask you somethin', cowboy," I began in my best Southern drawl. "Did y'all get y'alls' money upfront? Or do y'all have to complete the job first?"

"What difference does it make?" said the only black cowboy of the bunch.

"What difference does it make? If'n y'all didn't get paid upfront, y'all not gon' collect none of it." I looked at the first man. "Come and get some, tough guy." I stood perfectly still as he stepped within range. I needed to distract him. "So y'all fell for the longest straw trick, huh, sweet pea? Don't y'all know they just wanna see what I'm capable of doing before they approach me? What an idiot."

"Well, I'm gonna..."

Smack! Smack! Smack! Each blow of the three-punch combination sounded off in a fraction of a second. The Spaniard was stunned by the sheer speed of the blows. Blood trickled down both nostrils and out the corner of his mouth. I smiled. He didn't even see it coming.

"You little bit..."

Smack! Smack! Smack! I hit him three more times in rapid succession. His head snapped back with each blow. Every time he opened his mouth to say something, I was going to close it. "I don't like that word." I smiled.

"Damn, Tony," the black cowboy said. "She fuckin' you up. Get that bitch, man."

"Yeah, Tony," I joked. "I'm fuckin' you up. You'd better do something. This is about to get real embarrassin'."

Tony was on the verge of losing control. I could see the frustration in his face. After taking six quick humiliating punches to the face, I knew he was going to go on the offensive, which was exactly what I wanted him to do. I was one beat ahead of him when he attempted to hit me with his right. Just before he brought the hand up, I intercepted it, and moved in closer. He was about to throw the left. I was already intercepting it, moving closer still. Before he knew it, Smack! Smack! Smack! He dropped to one knee and I kicked him in the face.

While my foot was still in the air, I could hear the howl of a bullwhip coming at me. Woo, woo, woo. I turned and grabbed it just before the tail broke the sound barrier and crackled.

# CHAPTER 64

My plan was to snatch the whip out of his hand before he knew what had happened, but the howl of another whip and another was coming too fast for me to react. They both hit me in the back one right after the other. Right then, at that pivotal moment, I was transported back to the seventeenth century.

"Shhhhhhit!" I yelled, sucking in air through clenched teeth. I never felt anything like that in my life. The pain of the lash was penetrating. I felt the power of it in the marrow of my bones. My back arched all by itself. The rage of four hundred years began to swell within me. For the first time, I could really identify with Kunta Kinte. I was so enraged at that moment that I wanted to kill every last one of them.

Woo, woo, woo. Someone was about to hit me again and I was in too much pain to get out of the way. The tail of the whip broke the sound barrier and cracked loudly against my back. Woo, woo, woo.

Another one had unleashed his. Crack! I had been hit yet again. I felt like the helpless sheriff in the movie *High Plains Drifter* who was being beaten mercilessly by three men with bullwhips.

I took off running. They were going to beat me to death. Luckily for me they were having fun. Otherwise, I would end up in anti-gravity boots just like Sarah Lawford and Taylor Hoffman.

"Y'all can run, but y'all can't hide!" one of the men yelled out.

I could hear them laughing at me. It wasn't surface laughter either. It was deep belly laughing. The kind of laughter that made you double over and hold your stomach. These men were sadistic maniacs, I thought.

"Y'all know what we oughta do," Tony said between laughs. "We oughta get some of that pussy."

"Yeah! Let's pull a train on the bitch," one of the others said.

"Choo-choo!" another man yelled. "Ya hear that little lady? That's the train getting' ready to pull into yo' station."

"Yeah. There's four of 'em gettin' ready to pull in," Tony said, still laughing.

I grabbed Coco Nimburu's sword from its rack and faced my would-be rapists. Warm tears filled my eyes and dropped. I was more than angry. I had finally felt the humiliation that many other blacks talk about. Having grown up in China, my experiences were different.

I wasn't around during the civil rights era. I only read about it. And not because I wanted to, but because my father insisted that I read about Malcolm X, Dr. Martin Luther King Jr., H. Rapp Brown, and so many others. Now, over a decade later, I understood the quizzical looks of my Howard University classmates when I had said, "I haven't been discriminated against." Even though I knew the whipping wasn't racially motivated, the sting of the lash got my attention pretty damn quick.

And now, sword in hand, the thing that I feared most was not my life, but the taking of theirs. Truth be told, I had lost control. I wanted their heads for what they had done to me. Sweet Jesus, I said within. Please don't let me kill these muthafuckas.

"Y'all think that sword is gonna save y'all?" Tony asked rhetorically.

I remained focused when the three men with the whips came at me—all at the same time. I stepped into the midst of them, ready to take heads. Woo, woo, woo, the whips were coming. I sliced up. I sliced down and around. Clump, clump, clump. All three whips had been disabled, but I was still full of fury—deadly fury.

The men were backing off now that I had the upper hand. I went after Tony and he backed away. He kept backing away until he hit a steel pillar. The fear in his eyes was nothing short of complete and utter horror.

"Help me!" he screamed.

"Fuck that," the black one said. "You on yo' own, man. I'm outta here. It ain't worth it."

"Me, too," said another man. The two men fled.

I drew the sword back to take his good-for-nothing life when I was suddenly awakened from my crazed fury. The quality of peace I felt at that critical moment was like the meditation that I was experiencing prior to being intruded upon, only deeper. My eyes softened. I lowered the sword and backed away.

# CHAPTER 65

Terry and Jerry watched the two men blast through the entrance and run down the street. Stunned by what they were witnessing, they wondered what had happened in such a short amount of time. Surely four able-bodied men could handle one smallish woman, no matter how many self-defense classes she taught.

In their minds, only a few so-called martial artists could actually defend themselves in real combat. Their black belts were bought and paid for. Yes, they studied for three or four years. Some even taught classes, but most were living vicariously by the reputations of movie stars, who may not be able to defend themselves either.

"You know we have to pay them a visit, don't you, Terry?" Jerry asked.

"Yeah, but I'm more concerned with what's going on with the other two."

+++

I put the sword back in its sheath. I would continue the battle, but I would not take their lives. I would hurt them—seriously. But they will live. I turned to face my enemies who, for whatever reason, were still there. Quickly, I walked back into the center of the room, determined to give them a whipping they would never forget. Both men were closing in, ready to take the wind out of my sails.

"Grab her, Billy," Tony called out.

I let Billy snatch me by the shirt and pull me in. Using my thumb, I twisted his wrist in a direction that it wasn't meant to go in. He yelped in pain. I added more pressure. Then more pressure until I heard his wrist snap like a twig. Quickly, I grabbed the muscular arm with the broken wrist and twisted it until it too was broken. All of this happened in less than three seconds. I let him go and he took off, holding his arm as if it were in a sling.

I walked toward Tony. He backed up. "Be a man and fight," I said.

He was standing near the picture window that had my image and the words "The Dojo" painted on it. I threw my left hand straight up in the air to distract him. When he cut his eyes to see what I was doing with the hand, I moved in and attacked the lower part of his body with a straight punch. He blocked the punch rather easily, but it was too late. I was already in position to inflict whatever damage I wanted. I reversed the straight punch. He blocked that, too. I pulled his arm down and pounded his face with my fists, which left him dazed and disoriented. I grabbed his hand and started spinning him around until he was running. Then I let him go and he ran face first into a steel pillar. Blood was splattered against the pool and all over his face. While he struggled to regain his equilibrium, I hit him with a full blast thrust kick that caused him to leave his feet, fly through the glass window and land on the hood of Kelly's Stingray, which had just pulled up. I could hear George Duke's "Reach For It" blaring from her car.

I climbed through the shattered glass and pulled him to his feet. Smack! I hit him with a hard right. I drew back and hit him with another right. He tried to fall, but I wouldn't let him. Smack! Another right.

The loud stereo was suddenly silent. Kelly got out of her car. "Is this the Lasher, Phoenix?" she asked in a frenzied tone.

"No. He's just the hired help," I said. "But you're going to tell us who sent you, aren't you, Tony?" Smack! I hit him again. He fell up against the car. "Now, who sent you?"

Out of nowhere, an unheard bullet whistled past

me and entered Tony's skull, which exploded like a dropped watermelon. Tony was dead. Kelly and I took cover immediately alongside the Stingray. We looked around. Nothing was moving. Not even the insects. I listened for the start of an engine and never heard one.

"What the hell is going on, Phoenix?" Kelly asked.

"I think I may know who's behind the killings," I said.

# CHAPTER 66

The dojo was filled with FBI agents and police officers. Network reporters were on the scene retelling a story that I had lived. McGregor confirmed my suspicions. My attackers were not the men who were terrorizing women in the District of Columbia. The bull-whips were made of cowhide, not kangaroo. But more importantly, I now knew that we were much closer to them than we realized. The killers knew who I was and considered me a threat. Why else would they send four men to brutalize me?

"We found the other three men, Phoenix," Kortney Malone said when she walked into the office of my dojo. "Some of our guys found them a few blocks away with their heads blown to bits, just like the guy lying out on the concrete."

"Poor bastards," Kelly said sarcastically.

"They were sacrificial lambs, Kelly," I said. "The real killers were going to kill them anyway. They couldn't risk being exposed by four yahoos. They want to continue their mating ritual."

"Mating ritual?" Kortney questioned.

"I don't know what else to call it at this point," I said. "We know they rape the women and beat them savagely before dismembering them."

Kortney frowned. "Yeah, so?"

"Listen, this is just a hunch, but I think we've been spinning our wheels. I think Alexis Connelly hired a pair of serial killers to kill her father's wife who happened to be one of her best friends."

Kortney curled her lips. "And you think this because?"

"A couple of weeks ago, Dawn McNeil told us that Connelly was the woman who ran the prison library. We know that Dwight Rappaport was corresponding with someone who had access to the library computer."

"And?" Kortney folded her arms defiantly.

"And Connelly got out July fifth. A few weeks later, the bodies of Louis and Kathy Perkins were found. The warden's murder had nothing to do with drugs. Alexis is rich. She didn't need the money. That's why the killers didn't take the money and the cocaine." I paused to let my theory sink in a bit.

"Go on. You've got my attention," Kortney said, relaxing her arms.

"Not long after that, Malibu PD finds a blood-bath at the Connelly mansion," I went on.

"Even if she had Perkins killed, why kill her best friend?"

# CHAPTER 67

"Probably because she married her father," I said. "If I knew that, I would have come to you two weeks ago. With no motive, we're at a standstill. This case has had so many dead ends that I didn't completely trust the theory myself until a couple of hours ago."

"You should have said something two weeks ago," Kortney said forcefully.

"Perhaps I would have if you had shown you were a team player. All you ever talk about is weeding out the tare. Firing and suspending agents. To tell you the truth Kortney, if I hadn't been attacked, I wouldn't have even bothered now."

Kortney folded her arms again. "Well, why didn't you check it out on your own?"

"I did all I could do. No one has seen Alexis Connelly since she was released."

"What about her parole officer?"

"She's not on parole. She did her time and hasn't

been seen since," I said. "So what was I supposed to come to you with? Was I supposed to say I think a recently released prisoner with everything to lose and nothing to gain is having people killed?"

Kortney stared at me without blinking for about thirty seconds. "Phoenix, there's no need for the hostile tone. Now, what kind of prisoner was she?"

"Let me put it this way, Kortney, she was the librarian. You don't get in that position without being a model prisoner."

"Nothing on her record at all?"

"She was in for manslaughter. Killed her mother. It turns out that Alexis and her father were deeply in love. How sick is that? She killed her when she was sixteen. Assuming she's behind it, we have to build a case without her prior coming in. We won't be able to get search warrants or anything based on the manslaughter conviction. So, you see, it isn't as cut and dry as you think."

"Yes, I see," Kortney said with resignation. "And we have no idea where she is?"

"None."

"Tell her the rest, Phoenix," Kelly interrupted.

I frowned.

"What do you have?" Kortney asked.

"It's a long shot," I said.

"In spite of what you think, I am a team player,"

Kortney assured me. "Just tell me what you have. Theory or otherwise. If it's sound, we roll with it."

"Okay, but hear me out before you fly off the handle," I said, preparing her for an outlandish theory.

She nodded.

"Well, it's a collage of things, Kortney. Small, almost insignificant things. Everything began to click when I was meditating. I was thinking about the case and the evidence we'd collected. Then images started to flow together for some reason. I remembered Dwight Rappaport's hairless body. At first, I didn't think anything of it until the image of the woman in the *Sugar and Spice* video came to mind. The woman had no pubic hair. And she was being whipped by two women."

"So? What are you saying?"

"I'm saying we're looking for women, not men."

"But the victims were raped."

"That they were. Dwight Rappaport was a dealer in sex toys. We found a replica strap-on of his penis in his closet. Both Heather Connelly and Taylor Hoffman had all kinds of sex toys in their homes. Therefore, it isn't much of a reach to say that the sexual tastes of these women were a little exotic. According to Detective Thompson, the Malibu coroner found vaginal fluid in Heather Connelly's mouth. It came from Sandra Rhodes who was also murdered that night at the mansion."

"So we're talking about lesbian murderers?"

"Maybe. Could be bisexual. It's California. Who the hell knows out there?"

"Is there any more?" Kortney asked.

"Yes. The common link in all of this is the receipts; another overlooked item. Sarah Lawford and Season Chambers had both been to the Pennsylvania Avenue post office the day they were killed. I called the evidence room to confirm this. They had all been customers of a postal clerk named Geraldine. When we were looking for an address for Dwight Rappaport, she seemed nervous. She had a difficult customer just as we walked in. At the time, I assumed that was why she was agitated. I'm convinced she knows something. She had means and opportunity."

"What makes you so sure?"

"First off, Geraldine had access to Dwight Rappaport's box. She could have ordered the bullwhips and collected them when they came in. Rappaport wouldn't have even known about it. Who knows, she probably picked him when she saw what kind of mail he was getting and to cover her own tracks. Second, remember the video I mentioned? *Sugar and Spice*? They're a team. And

I would wager that her partner in crime is in an equally unassuming position. A position where they have access to addresses. Maybe the DMV, or something like that."

"So you really believe they're public servants?"

"How else do you explain the receipts? Assume for a second that Geraldine is in on it. If her partner is working for the DMV, she can get their driver's license numbers when her customers write a check. The other woman looks them up on the computer."

"I gotta be honest with you, Phoenix," Kortney began. "That's flimsy as hell. But pull the clerk in for questioning. Maybe you can rattle her cage."

"Something just occurred to me," I said in a distant voice. "My daughter was in a fight a couple of weeks ago. She was defending a little boy in the neighborhood. I'll never forget her answer when I asked her how many boys she'd fought with. She said, 'They were girls.'"

# CHAPTER 68

Catherine Spalding had gone to the Pennsylvania Avenue post office and given Geraldine Temperton one tongue-lashing too many. Catherine Spalding had always paid cash, but when the credit card system was down a couple of weeks ago, she was forced to write a check because she didn't have enough cash to cover the cost of the packages she wanted to ship.

Geraldine had patiently waited for that day to come. She knew it would sooner or later. That very evening, when she closed out her drawer, she carefully went through each and every check she took in that day, looking diligently for the check she'd received from her longtime agitator. Normally, Jerry, Geraldine Temperton; and Terry, Theresa Temperton, wouldn't bother with an old biddy like Catherine Spalding, but this was personal. It was indeed her turn to feel the sting of the lash.

The twins had picked their women from among the cream of the crop. In order to be chosen, Jerry had to actually serve a selected beauty that had come to her counter at the Pennsylvania Avenue post office. The same restrictions applied to the women that Terry served at the library where she worked. When a beautiful woman came to Terry's counter to check out an item, the computer automatically pulled up a screen that showed the woman's home address. Terry had chosen Phoenix when she served her and Savannah; before she learned that Phoenix was an FBI agent. That fact saved her from the twins.

Both twins were expert computer hackers. Jerry wrote down the driver's license number of potential victims when she accepted a check. With that number they were able to access DMV computers, attain social security numbers, pull credit reports, check police records, view airline manifests, examine bank accounts, and search just about any institution that kept computer records. They collected invaluable information on potential victims before deciding how and when they would die. Tonight it was Catherine Spalding's turn.

Jerry bent down and snatched Catherine Spalding by her crimson hair. "How does it feel? How does it feel to be humiliated?"

Catherine was naked and hanging upside-down in a pair of portable anti-gravity boots with her mouth taped shut. Gravity had caused her sixty-five-year-old flab to sag. She must have weighed in excess of two hundred pounds. It was a gross sight.

Catherine tried to talk but her words were muffled and incoherent. The sound of the whip howled through the air and cracked loudly against the flesh it struck. Her body convulsed violently. She began to shake uncontrollably for a few seconds and stopped all of a sudden.

Terry frowned. She moved closer, lifted her arm to take her pulse, and felt none. "I don't believe this. The old buzzard croaked."

Jerry screamed maniacally and beat on the old woman like a five-year-old having a temper tantrum. "You can't die! Not yet! Not yet, you old cow! Wake up!" Jerry hit her a few more times. "Wake your ass up!"

Terry laughed. "Let's go, Sis. She's done."

"No! I'm going to get my pound of flesh! She humiliated me too many times!"

# CHAPTER 69

The next morning I called the post office from Headquarters. If Geraldine was one of our killers, I didn't want to tip her off that we were on to her by paying another visit. She might have a weapon and start shooting innocent citizens. Kelly and I believed that our new suspect had sent the men who attacked me in my dojo. If we were right, if Geraldine was one of the killers, and if she sent those guys after me, she had killed them, which meant she was capable of mass murder. Either way, I wasn't going to risk it by showing up unannounced and flashing my credentials.

"Pennsylvania Avenue Post Office. Carl speaking," a man said after picking up the phone.

"This is Special Agent Phoenix Perry. FBI. I'm calling about one of your employees. I believe her name is Geraldine?" I dangled the name, hoping he would provide the last name without thinking.

"Geraldine Temperton?" he queried without thought.

"Yes. Unless you have more than one," I said, writing down her last name.

"Only one. What's this all about?"

"Is she working today?" I asked, ignoring his question. No need to alarm him on suspicion alone.

"Agent Perry, if you want information on my employees, you'd better come in and let me see some identification."

"Listen, Carl," I began, trying to be as friendly as possible. We were finally on to something and I didn't want to make an enemy by playing hard-ball. "I'd be happy to come down there and show you all the identification you want. However, Geraldine is a suspect in an ongoing case..."

"What kind of a case?" he interrupted.

"I can't tell you that, Carl. All I can tell you is that she's a suspect. And since I was just there a couple of weeks ago and spoke with her then, I'm sure she would recognize me. If she's there, I can meet you outside and show you my credentials."

Silence took over for a few seconds. "She called in. But if you want to know anything else, I'll need to see some ID."

"No problem. We'll be right down."

# CHAPTER 70

Sean Bellamy, flanked by two tough-looking men wearing dark shades and suits, entered the offices of the Drew Perry Investigative Firm.

"How may I help you?" asked Sherry Henderson, the high-cheek boned, walnut-skinned receptionist. She was sitting behind a circular desk covered with ceramic animals, pictures under fiberglass, red long-stemmed roses, a basket of fruit, a canister of peppermints, and a thirty-line phone.

Sean looked at her nameplate. "Hello, Sherry. I'm here to see Keyth Perry."

"Do you have an appointment?" the dark beauty inquired.

"No, but I'm sure he'll see me. Tell him Sean Bellamy is here."

Sherry stared at him intensely for a few seconds. He looked familiar but she couldn't place the face. "Excuse me, sir. But have we met?"

"No, we haven't." Sean smiled. "Perhaps you've

met my mother. That's her in the picture behind you with Sydney Drew."

Sherry turned around. "Yes. Okay. You look just like your mother minus the blonde hair." She hit a button on the phone and spoke into her headset. "Mr. Perry, Sean Bellamy is here to see you."

A minute later, Keyth Perry came out of his office and greeted Sean Bellamy and the four men walked into his office and closed the door. Gesturing with his hand, Keyth offered them a seat. Bellamy sat on the sofa but the two men with him continued standing.

Keyth couldn't help thinking about the stories that Phoenix had told him about Coco Nimburu and Adrienne Bellamy. He wondered how much Sean knew about the murders that had taken place a couple of months earlier.

"Can I get you a cup of coffee, Mr. Bellamy?" Keyth said.

"No, thanks. And call me Sean."

Keyth sat across from them on the mahogany love seat. He took a sip of coffee before saying, "Okay, Sean. What can Drew Perry do for you?"

"I need a favor," Sean said in a serious tone. "I need you to find a woman for me. I'll pay whatever you ask." He opened a silver briefcase and handed Keyth a photo. "Her name is Victoria Warren."

Keyth recognized the name immediately but didn't let on that he knew who the woman was and what their relationship had been. "Why are you looking for her, Sean?"

"I'm planning to marry her," Sean said confidently.

# CHAPTER 71

"What's this all about?" Keyth asked firmly. "I need to know everything before I commit the resources of this firm to an endeavor like that."

"I mean the woman no harm, I assure you. I intend to marry her, Keyth. We were seeing each other some years back and she broke the relationship off. She claimed she was pregnant by another man."

"Claimed?" Keyth questioned.

"Yes. Claimed."

"How do you know she wasn't telling the truth?"

"Well, as you no doubt know, my mother was killed by an assassin this past June and I took over the day-to-day operations of the Bellamy Empire. That's how I found out about Drew Perry. My mother helped your wife's father put this business together. Did you know that, Mr. Perry?"

Sean was trying to find out how much he knew about his mother's death and Keyth knew it. So he played along. "The part about your mother helping Sydney get his dream off the ground? Or the part about how you found out?"

Sean smiled and continued, "It turns out that my mother orchestrated the entire thing. There was no other man. The baby was mine."

"And you can prove this?"

"I have a signed contract."

"Do you have it with you?"

Sean handed the contract to Keyth, who quickly flipped to the signature page and read the names on the document. Sterling Wise was the attorney representing Adrienne Bellamy. Then he flipped back to the first page and began reading. The contract spelled out the conditions under which Victoria Warren and her family would be taken care of for the rest of their lives if she agreed to an abortion.

"Forgive me for asking, but why would you want to marry a woman who would sell out for money? If she did it once, she might do it again. How can you trust a woman like that?"

"Without going into a lot of detail, suffice it to say that Victoria was under tremendous pressure. My mother had purchased the mortgage on her parents' property. Then she had them both fired from their jobs. Victoria was working on her doctorate at Stanford when my mother had her dismissed on fraud charges. What other choice did she have?"

There were a lot of things she could have done, Keyth thought, but said none of them. What good would it do? The son was just like the mother. He was going to have his way no matter what.

"Sean, it's been a few years since this contract was signed. She could be seeing someone else by now. And given the recent tragic death of her parents, do you really think she would be receptive to you?"

"Let me worry about that, okay, Keyth? Now, will you take the case, or not?"

"Sure. I'll put my best man on it."

"Great. When can you begin?"

"It seems simple enough, Sean. Shouldn't take too long. We can begin immediately."

# CHAPTER 72

We had found them. When Kelly and I showed Carl our credentials, he was very cooperative. It turns out that Geraldine Temperton had a twin and they lived together in a spacious home on Vermont Avenue in Fairfax, Virginia.

Even though the Temperton twins were only suspects at this point, Kortney Malone thought we needed to get all the civilians out of the neighborhood before we went in. She didn't want them to take any hostages and try to negotiate their way out. I agreed with her. It was the smart thing to do.

By one p.m., we had set up a command post in a Chevy van filled with sophisticated electronic surveillance equipment a few houses down the street, out of visual range of the Temperton house. We had an assault team geared up and ready to go. But first, we needed to know if they were actually in the house. The last thing we wanted to do was kick in the door of an empty house and give away our hard-earned advantage.

Kelly suggested we call the house and pretend to be telemarketers. And if that didn't work, we could have an agent don a Federal Express uniform and go to the front door. Either way, we needed to do something immediately, before the media got wind of what we were doing.

"Make the call, Kelly," I said.

"Why me?"

"It was your idea." I laughed.

Kelly flipped open her cell. "What's the number?"

"I know you're not going to call on that cell," I said. "What if they have caller ID? It's going to show up as a cell."

"Fine. I'll use one of these." She picked up a headset on the control console of the command post. "What will these show?"

"It'll show up as unlisted," the tech said.

Kelly dialed the number. Three seconds later she hung up the phone.

"What happened?" I asked.

"They have privacy manager. You have to say who you are and what you want before they'll pick up the phone."

"I guess we go with the Federal Express idea," Kortney said.

"Can we tap into the post office line and call from there?" I asked the tech.

"Yes, but it will take some time to set up," he said. "We can climb the pole and tap in from there. We tell them we're the phone company and say they haven't paid the bill. We can at least find out if someone's there."

"Do it," Kortney said.

The tech left and walked down the street. A few minutes later the phone inside the command post rang. Kelly picked up.

"McPherson." She paused. "Go ahead. I'm ready."

She looked at me and mouthed, "It's ringing." "This is the phone company. May I speak with Geraldine Temperton?"

"This is her sister, Theresa. Is there a problem?"

"Yes. We haven't received a payment in three months. She's been a loyal customer and we'd hate to cut the service off without giving her a chance to catch her payments up."

"Jerry!" Theresa shouted. "Did you pay the phone bill?"

Kelly looked at us and smiled. Then she mouthed, "Both of them are there."

Geraldine picked up the phone. "Listen, I paid the bill. I have the canceled checks in my hand. There must be some mistake."

"What's your address, Ma'am?" Kelly asked.

"1619 Vermont."

"Ma'am, I apologize. We have you mixed up with another customer. We show the payments were on time for that address. Sorry for the inconvenience." Kelly hung up.

"We got 'em." I smiled. "Did they suspect anything?"

"Not that I could tell," Kelly said.

# CHAPTER 73

Two hours later, Geraldine and Theresa were downstairs in the basement working out, where they had a complete Olympic weight set, including an assortment of dumbbells, barbells, a treadmill, a stairmaster, jump rope, a heavy bag and a stationary bike.

Geraldine was spotting Theresa, who was bench pressing two hundred seventy-five pounds. She had already pressed the weight ten times on her way to fifteen. The weight felt heavier and heavier as she approached her goal.

"Come on, Sis," Geraldine encouraged. "One more."

Theresa pressed as hard as she could, finally getting the enormous amount of weight back up over her chest. She was lifting nearly twice her weight. The twins were over six feet tall and weighed a lean one hundred sixty-five pounds.

"One more, Sis. One more."

Theresa lowered the bar to her chest and again she pressed it upward, struggling to get it back up.

"Push! Harder! Harder!" Geraldine urged.

The bar eased up further and further until she had the bar over her chest again. She held the bar there and took a few deep breaths. "I'm going to need your help with this last one, Jerry."

"Let me know when you're ready."

"I'm ready," Theresa said and lowered the bar.

She tried to lift the bar again, but could barely get it up. Geraldine grabbed the bar with both hands and helped Theresa lift. "Now for the burn, Sis. Five more. I'll help you get it up."

Just as they finished the burn, the phone rang. Geraldine answered. "Hello."

"This is Special Agent Phoenix Perry of the FBI. We have the house surrounded. Come out with your hands up and you won't be harmed."

# CHAPTER 74

Theresa froze. Her mind filled with questions. *How did they find us? Had the Connelly twins sold us out? Was Catherine Spalding alive? Did she faint? Had she played us for fools last night? How did they get our number?* Then it occurred to her that the earlier call from the phone company had actually been the FBI checking to see if both of them were in the house.

"Am I speaking with Geraldine or Theresa?" Phoenix said. "You girls have a chance at walking away with your lives if you cooperate. I don't want to kill anyone today."

"What makes you think we want to live?" Theresa laughed sardonically.

Phoenix paused. She hadn't counted on that response. "Point taken."

"But...if we surrender, what are we looking at? The chair?"

Sarcastically, Phoenix said, "If I had to guess, I'd

say you two are looking at life without the possibility. But that's just a guess."

"Aren't you supposed to try and talk us out, Agent Perry? Sounds like you want a fight. Is that what you want? You want a shootout? 'Cause if you do, we can provide one."

"Nobody wants a shootout, okay? But there's no way you're going to get away. We have the house surrounded and all the roads are blocked. Now...are you two really prepared to die?"

"We need time to think about it."

"I'll give you thirty minutes. After that, we're coming in. It's your choice." She hung up the phone.

+++

"This is about to get dicey," I said. "They're prepared to shoot it out."

"Why antagonize the situation, Phoenix?" Kortney asked.

"I needed to know what our people were up against," I explained. "We could have sent our guys in there unsure of their intentions. They're cornered and they know it. They've got nothing to lose. And if I have to push a little to see what their thinking is, that's what I'm going to do."

"If they have nothing to lose, why are we waiting?" Kelly asked.

"I gave them thirty minutes," I said.

"We don't owe them anything, Phoenix. They could have an arsenal in there. And if they do, in thirty minutes we could run into a buzz saw. I say we send them in now and surprise 'em."

"It's your call, Phoenix," Kortney said. "But I think we give them the thirty minutes. We need to be shark sure when we go in. I think it would be better in the long run to wait them out. They're not going anywhere. Sooner or later, they're going to fall asleep and we can take them then. You do want them alive, don't you, Phoenix? Or do you want to even the score for Sarah Lawford's murder?"

"I won't even dignify that with a response," I scowled. Then I picked up the radio. "Assault team leader, are your people in position?"

"Affirmative. We are good to go. Awaiting further instructions."

"Sit tight. We need them alive," I said.

"Have you looked at the sky lately? A storm is coming. It could impair our vision. I don't want any of my people to get caught in our own crossfire if the suspects decide to shoot their way out."

"I understand your concern, but we need these two alive. Let's not rush this thing. They have vital information on another suspect. We'll deal with the rain when we need to."

"Understood. Standing by."

✛✛✛

"They're coming in," Geraldine whispered. She picked up paper and a pen and wrote: *They're probably listening, Sis. We better gear up. We've only got thirty minutes, if that.*

Theresa wrote: *If we get the thirty, we can be sure they're going to shut off the electricity when the time expires. Let's stick to the plan.*

Geraldine wrote: *Let's get everything we need upstairs and turn on some music so we can talk in private.*

Theresa wrote: *I think I should call the media now. You start bringing up the stuff.*

Geraldine nodded.

# CHAPTER 75

The twins had a contingency plan for the FBI. But for it to work, they needed time. Time the FBI wouldn't give them. In less then twenty minutes, they would be coming through the doors—guns blazing.

Theresa Temperton sprinted up the basement stairs and into the kitchen, where her cellular phone was recharging. She picked up a notebook, which had the telephone numbers for CNN, ABC, NBC, CBS, and WSDC, Season Chambers' station. She didn't know how many she could call before the authorities caught on.

Just as she was about to make the first call, it occurred to her that she needed to close all the blinds. There would definitely be snipers. She did so as quickly as she could.

Geraldine ran up the stairs and dropped ammo clips on the kitchen floor. Just as quickly as she ran up, she was on her way back down. Theresa picked up the stereo remote control and turned on the stereo. Bon Jovi's "Dead or Alive" began.

The first call was to WSDC. "This is Theresa Temperton. My sister and I are responsible for the death of Season Chambers and quite a few others. My house is surrounded by FBI agents. So, if you want to scoop the networks, you'd better get to 1619 Vermont Avenue, Fairfax, Virginia in fifteen minutes. They're coming in." Theresa hung up the phone and called the remaining networks.

"Are you getting anything yet?" I asked the tech.

"Nothing since one of them said, 'They're coming in.'"

"What are they doing?"

"I can't tell. There was lots of movement. But they've turned the music up; I can't hear much now. It's like they know we're listening."

"The electric company will be here soon. We'll take care of the power then."

"I don't like this, Phoenix," Kortney said.

"I don't either," Kelly agreed.

"It's been almost thirty minutes," the assault team leader said. "Are we a go, or what?"

"Stand by," I said.

"I say we send them in now while we can still surprise them," Kelly offered. "Who knows what they're doing in there. You heard the tech. If they know we're listening, they could be setting booby traps or something."

"McPherson's right, Phoenix," Kortney said. "I still don't like it, but if we don't go in now, we might be sorry later."

"Come on guys," the assault team leader said. "We're about to lose our window of opportunity."

"Didn't I tell you to stand by?" I yelled into the radio. I was under tremendous pressure. If this went bad, it would set the advancements that women had made in the bureau back twenty years. And Kortney could forget about a permanent position as FBI director. They might have us all fetching coffee like the good ol' days.

"Yeah, but..." the team leader began.

I cut him off. "Then don't do jack until you hear from me! You got that!"

There was a long silence before the mic keyed. "Affirmative."

I was sure he was calling me all sorts of names, but I didn't care. I had more important things on my mind. I closed my eyes and tried to block out everything. Deep down, I believed I was right to wait. Theresa had told us they were prepared for a shootout. And I don't think she was bluffing. I didn't want to put the assault team in danger, but they had practiced this sort of thing thousands of times. I decided to go in.

"Team leader, this is the SAC. Prepare for a full breach on my command."

"On your command," he repeated.

Just as I was about to key the mic, an agent opened the van door and said, "Phoenix, you might want to hold off. The media's here."

"Which one?" I asked.

"All of them."

I shook my head slowly and curled my lips. "Team leader, this is the SAC. Stand down. I say again, stand down."

# CHAPTER 76

We moved the van closer to the Temperton house. They knew we were here. No need to hide. I looked out the tinted window of the van. The music in the house was still playing so we had no idea of what they were doing. With all the shades drawn, our sniper had nothing to shoot at. I wouldn't admit it, but I was glad the media showed up. I didn't want to go in anyway.

With the networks watching, filming everything, we had to be very careful. After all, this was a chance for them to up the price of a thirty-second spot during what they might call "Showdown in Fairfax" or something that would catch the viewers' attention. Besides, the last thing I wanted was a shootout with two desperate women—no matter what their crimes were.

The story was being broadcast on all the networks. The television screens in our van showed ID photos of Geraldine and Theresa Temperton they had acquired from their jobs. As the newsanchors filled the audience in on their crimes to date, pictures of each victim were displayed along with their occupations. They had assembled expert psychologists and lawyers, who debated their sanity and what legal strategy would be most effective. It was sickening. Nevertheless, I was amazed at how quickly they could get background information, and pictures of all the victims.

Just as I knew they would, the news anchors began to assign blame. In a subtle, almost undetectable way, they blamed everybody except the women who had committed the crimes. CNN was doing a special *Talk Back Live*. A caller asked, "How can Geraldine work for the postal service and have a criminal record?"

A lawyer answered, "Her record as a juvenile was sealed. Whatever crimes she committed as a juvenile couldn't be held against her when she applied for the job. In fact, because her records were sealed, the postal service had no way of knowing her juvenile record. On top of that, her records can't be found. We only know what we know through word of mouth, which incidentally wouldn't stand up in a court of law."

The moderator of *Talk Back Live* couldn't resist

the opportunity to bring up past postal shootings. On a split screen was a list of every postal shooting in the country and the number of victims.

After that, the moderator asked, "What's happened to American women? Have they taken equal rights too far?"

I knew it was only going to get worse when I read the question at the bottom of the screen. "What impact does race have on mass murder?" I bet they made a bundle on that question alone. People were going to tune in just to hear the responses. I shook my head in disgust.

The phone rang in the van. The call was coming from inside the Temperton house. I heard one of the Temperton girls say, "Have you guys forgotten about us?"

# CHAPTER 77

"No," I said.

"Thought you hotshots were coming in to get us."

"We'll be coming—don't worry. It'll be in our time, not yours," I said and muted the television. "In the meantime, tell me how you know Alexis Connelly."

"First, tell me how you found us?"

"Who am I speaking with? Sugar or Spice?"

"We're both on the phone. This is Jerry, but you can call me Sugar if you like. I can be very sweet. Want a taste?" She laughed. "Theresa likes to be called Terry."

"I guess that's a dyke thing, huh?"

"Agent Perry, do you know how close you came to being one of our captives?" Terry asked.

"Captives? Is that what you call the women you brutalize, rape, and dismember?"

Terry ignored my question and went on talking as if she didn't hear me. "Remember taking that adorable daughter of yours to the library a couple of weeks back?"

"Yes," I said in horror.

"When I mentioned you to my sister, she told me you were an FBI agent. If we had been identical twins, you would have recognized me. We let you live because we didn't need the heat. So tell us how you found us."

"A combination of luck and skill. When we found Rappaport, he was watching a skin flick called *Sugar and Spice*. We found a replica of the Plow you girls like to use on your victims in his closet, but what led us back to you, Geraldine, was the receipts."

"The receipts?" Terry repeated. "What receipts?"

In a deprecating tone, Geraldine said, "I'm sorry, Sis. I forgot all about the receipts."

I listened to the sisters talk.

"What receipts are you talking about?" Terry asked.

"The receipts we give to customers have our first names on them. And I forgot all about that. I got careless."

"Don't worry about it, Sis." Terry consoled. "We knew they were going to find us sooner or later."

"Excuse me," I interrupted. "Now that we're all getting along, tell me about Alexis Connelly."

"We met her at Norrell," Terry began. "She was

a fragile thing, but a straight lesbian all the way. She had to be ganged by the Deuces a few times before she fell into a routine. Tried to escape. That's when the guards started raping her. She told the warden and he got a piece, too. Kinda lost it after that. You could tell she wasn't all there to begin with. Had special medication and everything."

"Is that why she killed Warden Perkins and his wife? Because he raped her?"

"Alex didn't kill the warden," Jerry admitted. "We did. Me and Terry."

"So she hired you to do it?"

"You might say we did it out of gratitude," Terry said.

"Gratitude? So, she didn't hire you? She didn't ask you to kill for her? You did it as a thank-you gesture?"

"Yes," Jerry agreed. "What you have to understand is that Terry and I are poor white trash. Alex Connelly was rich. We helped her enhance the library computer system, and she wiped out our records with a few keystrokes. We owed her something for that."

"Why didn't you just stay out of jail? Wouldn't that have been thanks enough? You both had well-paying jobs with benefits and you threw them away."

"You can't change who you are any more than

we could change who we are," Terry barked. "Spare us the self-righteous attitude. Prison changes you, okay, Agent Perry. The things that we did to women. The things they did to us. You don't know what freedom is until you've spent a few years confined with sex-crazed women. Prison is the only place left in America where slavery is allowed and, dare I say, encouraged. You have two choices in the penal system. Take or be taken. Now...are you coming in to get us, or do we have to come out there and get you?"

I asked, "If prison is so liberating, why are you willing to die, rather than go back?"

"Because we've outgrown that kind of freedom," Jerry said. "Prison would be a setback for us now. Out here, we've had the freedom to pick a new captive at will. We've had the freedom to drive nice cars, live in a nice home, eat good food. No. We could never go back to Norrell. Never! It's too limiting. No variety. No spontaneity. No makeup. No perfume. Just hardened prison women. Who wants that? Besides, they might try to enslave us."

"So where's Alexis Connelly now?"

"Right under your nose."

With that, they hung up.

# CHAPTER 78

A strong breeze had cooled off the blistering summer in mere moments, which was accompanied by an unrelenting thunderstorm that dumped recycled water on our vehicle by the bucketful. The rain sounded like small pieces of hail pelting the van. Lightning flashed and lit up the darkening sky. The Temperton house was growing darker as time passed. We would be going in soon.

It had been a little over a month since we began our investigation and we were just a hundred feet from two of the most ruthless killers I had ever crossed paths with. I couldn't help wondering why the media was rehabilitating them. The Temperton twins had dismembered people while they were still alive, yet the media kept talking about how they were raised by an absentee father and a crack-addicted mother. Maybe there was something wrong with me. Perhaps being reared in another culture had taught me to punish the guilty.

I had given the order to cut power to the house a few hours earlier. It was approaching nine p.m. My cell rang. It was my husband calling. "Hello."

"How's it goin'?" Keyth said.

"It won't be long now. We'll be going in when they fall asleep."

"Guess who came into the office today?"

"Who?"

"Sean Bellamy."

# CHAPTER 79

"Oh really? What did he want?"

"He wanted to hire the firm."

"Hire the firm to do what?"

"He came into the office today with two body-guards. Two brothas. Bruisers, both of them. Clean-shaven. Looked like ex-military to me. Anyway, he wants us to find Victoria Warren."

Surprised, I said, "Why?"

"Says he plans to marry her. He found the contract she signed a few years back. Apparently his mother forced her to sign it with a number of different threats."

"Are you sure, Keyth? You sure it isn't some trick? The apple doesn't fall far from the tree."

"He seemed sincere enough. Said he was going to be runnin' for president."

"And he thinks marrying a black woman is going to help him win?" Everybody in the van stopped what they were doing and looked at me. I didn't mean to say that, but it slipped out. "So are you going to San Francisco, Keyth?"

"No. I'll just put somebody on it. Somebody I can depend on to do a good job."

"So he thinks she's going to marry him?"

"Yep."

I looked at the tech. He had his headphones on, listening to Sugar and Spice. I wondered what they were saying that was so interesting. I picked up the thermal scanner and looked at the house. I could see the body heat of the two women in a sixty-nine position. I frowned. Were they doing what I think they were doing? If the look on the tech's face was an indicator, they were. I swear I'll never understand why men find two women together so alluring.

"Keyth, let me call you later."

# CHAPTER 80

Three hours later, the two sisters had fallen asleep on the floor after a short session of vigorous lovemaking. We could hear them snoring. The tech had listened gleefully to the entire interlude. He wanted to use the thermal scanner to complete his voyeuristic adventure but I wouldn't let him. For all I knew, we were going to kill these two women. If they wanted to use their last hours on earth to do something perverse, so be it. But someone had to listen just in case, and I wasn't interested.

It was time to go in, but I was still hesitant. I knew that when they went in, no matter how careful the team was, if the women were able to grab a weapon, the assault team would have to shoot them.

Reluctantly, I picked up my handheld radio. "All units, move into position." I looked through the tinted glass of the van. Twelve agents wearing night-vision goggles, dressed in fatigues and flack jackets, ran across the street through the torrential downpour. Puddles of water splashed when their combat boots landed hard against the pavement underneath. Six went to the front door and six to the back. A minute later both units checked in.

"Unit one in position."

"Unit two in position."

"SAC, this is the team leader. We are in position and good to go. Awaiting further instructions."

"Standby, team leader," I said. I looked at the tech, who was still listening. "Are they still asleep?"

He nodded.

I picked up the thermal scanner and looked at their body heat silhouette. No movement.

"Team leader, you are a go. Be advised, the suspects are still sleeping, still in the front of the house," I said.

"Team leader to all units, we are a go on my command. Remember, we need them alive if possible." He paused. "Go!"

I heard both the back and front doors being kicked in. Suddenly the lights in the house switched on and loud music began playing.

"Oh, no," I said.

# CHAPTER 81

The lights blinded the agents. Paul McCartney's "Live and Let Die" blared and the loud music disoriented them. The twins had played possum. They had faked everything. They hadn't made love, and they definitely weren't asleep. They had lain perfectly still for over an hour, fully clothed, wearing flack jackets of their own. Then at precisely the right moment, Terry hit a switch that was connected to a portable generator that turned on the lights and music.

The twins picked up their weapons and fired. The agents jerked in response to the armor-piercing bullets that tore through their flack jackets and riddled their unsuspecting bodies. They screamed loudly as each bullet ripped through flesh and bone, hitting arteries, lungs, and other vital organs. Their blood flowed freely and covered the floor.

# CHAPTER 82

**W**e heard gunfire! They had tricked me. I knew something was wrong, but this was the furthest thing from my mind. Good thing DCPD was there backing us up. Kelly and I hopped out of the van into the pouring rain, wearing our FBI windbreakers—weapons drawn. We were carrying 9mms. No match for the automatic weapons we heard being fired inside the Temperton house.

Suddenly the lights were off again and the music stopped playing. As the police converged on the house, the twins came running out with a Tec-9 in each hand. When they squeezed the triggers, the barrels lit up the front yard. Bullets whistled past us and hit the surveillance vehicle, the police cars, and several of the media vans. Kelly and I took cover behind a couple of abandoned squad cars and returned fire.

Several officers were down. Others were in severe

pain. I could hear them crying out for help. It was difficult to see in the rain, but the flashes of light from the automatic weapons made it easier to spot the twins. Kelly grabbed the 12-gauge out of the squad car and squeezed off a couple of rounds.

I changed clips and waited. I knew they would have to reload soon. That would be my best chance at taking one of them. In the back of my mind, I knew I needed them alive but they had superior firepower. It was us or them. And I wasn't ready to die.

I heard a clip ricochet off the cement. I looked at Kelly. She heard it too. We nodded at each other. We both stood up and fired. We hit the same twin. She went down.

The other twin had run to a car and started it. She was backing up. The twin that we shot was on her feet, running toward the car. We shot at them again. The twin behind the wheel stuck her weapon out the window and shot at us. We took cover again.

I grabbed the hand-held radio off my belt. "All units, be advised, the twins are going east on Vermont in a late-model Ford Focus. Do not let them through. Protect yourselves, gentlemen. Even at the risk of killing them. They're wearing vests."

We fired round after round into the car while we pursued the twins on foot. Up ahead, I could see officers in the middle of the intersection behind their squad cars. They were firing also.

Suddenly I could hear the constant sound of the horn blowing as the car swerved off the street onto the sidewalk and over a fire hydrant. Water shot into the air and splashed down like an oversized drinking fountain. The car continued rolling at a slow pace until it rolled into a tree.

When I got to the car, I saw Geraldine Temperton sitting in the passenger seat with a Tec-9 under her chin, squeezing the trigger. I grabbed the weapon out of her hand and pulled her out of the car. I held her face down in the rain-drenched street and cuffed her. I looked back into the car at Theresa Temperton. Her face had been blown off. I cringed when I saw her. Bits of the windshield were buried in her face.

The situation had gone real bad, real quick. But we had gotten a gigantic break. A break that would save jobs after this fiasco. We had caught one of the killers. Geraldine was still alive, which meant we still had a chance to apprehend Alexis Connelly.

# CHAPTER 83

The tech was dead. So were at least ten agents and a few police officers. Several were hanging on to life by a thread. Kortney Malone had taken several bullets in the chest. She was hurt badly, but the rescue worker assured me she would live. For that, I was grateful. Malone would be good for the bureau.

I had known something was wrong. I could feel it. But there was no way to know that they had planned to ambush the FBI. Nevertheless, I felt responsible for what happened. What made matters worse was that it was all televised.

Kelly tried to console me, but I made the call. It didn't matter that we all wanted to go in. I made the call. It was on me. Agents were dead. Fortunately, no civilians were hit with all the stray bullets flying around.

The only good thing to come out of the fiasco was that we had captured one twin, and killed another.

Hopefully, Geraldine Temperton would help us find Alexis Connelly, who had mysteriously disappeared. We had to get a lead from Geraldine. Something—anything that would lead to her arrest and subsequent incarceration.

Mercifully, the thunderstorm that had soaked us was now over. There must have been eight EMS trucks in front of the Temperton house. I stood in the street watching one of them cart Kortney Malone off to Washington Memorial.

Kelly and I put on a pair of surgical gloves and went into the Temperton house. We needed to find something that would lead us to Alexis Connelly. We would question Geraldine later. Hopefully she'd want to make a deal.

In the living room, on the floor, we found a battery-powered tape recorder. I pushed the play button and we heard the twins snoring. I shook my head. We had been seriously duped.

Next to the living room fireplace, there was a liquid-cooled Yamaha diesel generator capable of delivering up to sixty-five hundred watts of electricity. There were several lines of electricity from the generator to the lights and the stereo system. The Temperton twins were smart. They knew we would come in with night-vision goggles. Turning on the lights had blinded them and the loud music made it impossible to hear. My anger simmered.

As if they were left for us to find, two red and black bullwhips lay on the couch, coiled as if they were snakes ready to strike. Perhaps I should've been happy, but it was too little too late. Finding the bullwhips wasn't like realizing the receipts were the keys to the killings. Finding the bullwhips now was more like a consolation prize. Thanks for playing, Bozo! Take this booby prize and go home.

I went over to the couch and picked one up. Flashes of what had happened to me at my dojo filled my mind. My face contorted when I saw myself being beaten. I can only imagine what the other women must have gone through. The coroner had said the savage beatings must have gone on for over an hour.

"Kelly," I said, "we have to make them pay for this."

# CHAPTER 84

The Connelly twins had watched the story break on the news like the rest of the country. Detailed reports had been given on how impossible it was for the Temperton twins to escape. They had shown all the roadblocks and had even talked to several uniformed officers. However, none of that would deter the Connellys from rescuing Geraldine Temperton.

They had waited all evening in a fully loaded Hummer with an extended bumper, monitoring the built-in television and police scanner. The WSDC helicopter had been providing aerial photos of the Tempertons' neighborhood all evening. They could possibly watch the vehicle that was taking Geraldine Temperton to FBI Headquarters.

From the drop-down, flat-screen television, they could see the vehicle that the FBI had put Geraldine Temperton into. The helicopter followed the vehicle as it drove away from the accident scene. The twins were moving parallel with the FBI vehicle.

Alexis floored it. She wanted to get several blocks ahead of the FBI so she could cut them off. The WSDC helicopter was still following—still filming the FBI car. Alexis parked the Hummer and turned off the headlights. She watched the television screen and waited patiently for the car to get closer. As the car approached the intersection, Alexis pressed hard on the gas pedal. The tires spun. Rubber burned.

The Hummer slammed hard into the side of the car and threatened to topple it. The twins grabbed their Styer Aug rifles and hopped out of the Hummer. They stood point-blank in front of the FBI car and sprayed the agents with bullets.

Alexis reached into the car, fumbled through the driver's blood-soaked pockets and grabbed the handcuff keys. She reached for the door handle but the frame of the car was bent and the door wouldn't open. Using the butt of her Styer Aug, she smashed the rear window, stretched inside, and uncuffed Geraldine.

"Let's go!" Alexis yelled. "I've got a plane waiting for us."

"No! We're going back!" Geraldine screamed. "They killed Jerry! I'm going to kill them!"

"Fine! We'll get them later!" Alexis offered. "We gotta go. Now!"

+++

Agent Perry," I heard someone say on my hand-held radio. "Turn the television on! Your prisoner is escaping!"

"What channel?" I asked.

"Thirteen."

Kelly turned on the TV and switched to Channel 13. WSDC's helicopter was reporting live from the escape scene. We saw Geraldine and Alexis Connelly having what appeared to be a no-holds-barred argument. They were only a couple of miles from the Temperton house. Just as we were about to run out of the house, Alexis raised her rifle and shot Geraldine point blank in the chest.

Alexis Connelly was still shooting Geraldine Temperton by the time we arrived. As far as I could tell, Geraldine was dead, but Alexis continued to fire into her corpse. Pow! Pow! Pow!

"Freeze, Connelly!" I yelled. Our 9mms were pointed at her.

She looked back at me over her shoulder. "She lied to us. I'm going to kill her."

Kelly and I looked at each other and frowned. What was she talking about? There was no one else on the scene. We looked around, wondering who was lurking in the shadows.

"Finish her, Alex," we heard Alexis say.

Kelly and I looked at each other again. It was clear now. Alexis Connelly was a schizophrenic. I lowered my weapon and whispered, "Keep her covered, Kelly. She's wearing a vest. Shoot to kill if you have to," I said. I wanted to take her alive. After everything that had happened that night, all the murders, somebody had to be taken into custody. Alexis Connelly was the only killer left.

"Alexis," I called in an even calm voice, "she's dead."

Pow! She fired into her again. "I know," Alexis said. "It's not my fault she died before I ran out of bullets." Pow! Pow! Click! "Now, we're ready to go with you, Agent Perry."

# CHAPTER 85

**B** ack at FBI headquarters, we were about to take Alexis Connelly's statement. The camera and tape recorders were on. Files filled with before and after photographs of the victims she and the Temperton twins had killed were sitting right in front of me. I was going to use them if she didn't confess fully and completely. I don't know how much good the pictures would do, but I had them there nevertheless.

Kelly and I sat on one side of the table, Connelly on the other. She looked strangely familiar, but I couldn't place her face anywhere. She seemed calm, almost serene. Connelly was slender with shoulder-length brunette hair and green eyes. There was nothing threatening about her at all. In fact, she looked perfectly normal, like any other citizen. I took a sip of my tea and reminded myself that this woman had raped, whipped, and dismembered a string of women.

"Should we tell them, Sam?" Alexis asked. "Or should we wait for our lawyers?"

Kelly and I looked at each other. I had heard about schizophrenia. I had even seen movies about it. But it's a different story watching it up close and personal.

"Might as well tell 'em, Alexis," the other voice said. "Tell her how you sat right across the aisle from her on the plane. Tell her how you only talked to her to keep her from asking too many questions once you recognized her."

I tried to remember the woman I had talked to, but the memory was hazy. The plane trip home seemed like a lifetime ago. Each time she spoke, she was looking directly into my eyes. Her green eyes were soft, showing no evidence of the homicidal maniac that lived within. I had just witnessed her handiwork. She had killed Geraldine Temperton and continued to shoot her long after she was dead.

"She doesn't want to hear about that, Sam," Alexis said. "She wants to know how all this began. Don't you? Isn't that what you wanna know? How this began?"

I nodded. I figured it would be best to let her talk if that's what she wanted to do. If I did, she would spill it all without having to trick or threaten her.

"Ever have sex with your father, Agent Perry?"

I tried not to frown. I wanted to appear as though what she had just asked was a normal question. Like asking me if I had eaten.

"No. I haven't," I said, hiding my absolute disgust. "Is that why you killed your mother, Alexis? She was trying to break you two up for her own selfish reasons?"

"Yes," Sam said. "My father had outgrown her. He needed me. We were truly in love and she had to go and ruin it."

"Ruin it how?"

"She was using the relationship to squeeze more money out of my father. I wasn't going to have it. So I did what I had to do."

I felt my stomach starting to turn. This woman had no moral compass whatsoever. No remorse. No sense of right and wrong.

"Tell us about Heather Connelly, Sandra Rhodes, and Paula Stevens," Kelly interjected.

"Heather was my girlfriend," Alexis said. "We were all intimate. But Heather got greedy. We were going to share everything with her when we got out. My father was lonely when we went to jail. And that greedy tart took advantage of him. She started fixing her hair like mine. Bought green contacts. Always hangin' around him. What was he to do? He's a man." She paused for what appeared to be a moment of reflection. "You know what? If she had treated him right, we would have let it slide. But she didn't. She started having wild cocaine parties and having drug dealers in the house. Heather was spending money like there was no tomorrow. To make matters worse, we tried to escape and our sentences were lengthened. Nothing our lawyers could do about it either. When our father learned that we wouldn't be home for a total of ten years, he started to fade away. Eventually blew his brains out."

I almost felt sorry for Alexis, but as she spoke, her eyes became cold—steel-like. Perhaps if she'd shown some contrition, I could've felt sorry for her loss, such as it was.

Out of nowhere, she started to laugh hysterically. "Tell 'em about the boyfriend, Alex."

Alex laughed. It was a totally different kind of laughter than Sam's. "We caught her in bed with some clown. We were going to kill them both until we overheard them talking about a foursome. She had replaced me with him. We girls used to have four-ways occasionally. Sometimes five with Taylor."

"Taylor Hoffman?" I asked.

"The one and only," one of them said. I was losing track. "So, anyway we waited in the guesthouse. And when they were into the act, we barged in. Threw her lover over the cliff. We went back to the house and some jeweler and a rent-a-cop show up with a diamond choker and matching earrings that the boyfriend had bought Heather with our money. Would you believe she had the nerve to give that clown a credit card? We sent the jeweler and the rent-a-cop over the cliff, too. Screamed all the way down. It's the kinda thing you look back on and laugh."

I took a sip of my tea and fought the urge to beat them both within an inch of their miserable lives. But I needed to know what Taylor Hoffman had to do with all of this. She didn't figure in at all.

"Tell us about Taylor Hoffman," I said.

"Her name used to be Bradshaw. We did her, too. Turned her out. She wanted to be a part of our group so we told her she had to do us. Heather, Paula, and Sandra, too. She thought she could leave our family. She was right here in Washington. You think she visited us? When we got sent away after we did our mother, she thought she was better than us. Then she met Jack Hoffman and pretended she didn't go both ways when she knew she liked women."

"So, that's why you killed her?" Kelly asked shaking her head in disbelief. "Because she didn't wanna be a part of your little family?"

Connelly laughed from her belly again. "Can you

think of a better reason to off somebody? What do you want? She was a freak."

Connelly stared at me lustfully. I got the feeling that she wished she could shackle me in a pair of anti-gravity boots and beat me into submission.

"You found her play things, didn't you, Agent Perry? You found her toys in her dresser drawer, didn't you? All kinds of creams and lubricants and candied panties and all sorts of interesting gadgets."

The Connelly twins went on and on. Switching from one personality to the other. After awhile, they talked to themselves as if we weren't even in the room. I'd never seen anything like it. Alexis Connelly wasn't even aware of the fact that Kelly and I had left the room. We kept the cameras rolling for about three hours and she never stopped talking.

Just when I thought I'd seen it all, an argument broke out. Sam accused Alex of being too soft and said they never would have been caught if Alex had listened to her. As the argument intensified, they started screaming at each other. One of them, and I don't dare guess who, started barking with the ferocity of a Doberman pinscher. That's when I walked out.

# EPILOGUE

Weeks had passed, and Alexis Connelly was safely locked away in a hospital for the criminally insane. She could have gotten away clean if she hadn't tried to save Geraldine Temperton. Fortunately for us, her loyalty was the one thing that brought her out of hiding and into our hands. If it weren't for little idiosyncrasies like that, it would be very difficult to catch criminals who take the time to plan their crimes.

I was lying in our bed while my husband applied cocoa butter to the wounds I had sustained from the whipping I had taken. It was time to reopen my dojo. I told Luther Pleasant that he would be my first student. He was so happy. I'd already ordered his uniform. He was going to be a good student. I could tell about some people right off. He had the desire and there was no telling how far he would go, or how fast.

My husband was telling me about the reunion of Victoria Warren and Sean Bellamy. Apparently, they were going to marry, which I found ironic, considering what his mother had done to prevent it. Love is like that, I guess. No matter what you do, two people will love each other through the best and worst of times.

"I'm thinking of voting for Bellamy," Keyth said and put the cap back on the cocoa butter."

I turned over and faced him. "Really? And why is that?"

"For one reason, I'm sick of both the Democrats and the Republicans. The Democrats laud the Kennedy brothers and Dr. King as their icons; yet, you never hear them say what those men said. For example, John Kennedy said, 'Ask not what your country can do for you, but what you can do for your country.' And Dr. King said, 'Judge by the content of their character.' Do you ever hear Democrats say that? No, you don't. It's a different party.

"I thought you liked the Republicans, Keyth. You still believe in self-reliance, don't you?"

"Of course I do. My problem with the Republicans is the same problem I have with a number of white people."

"And what's that?"

"There aren't enough whistleblowers in the party. One day, one of them is going to slip up and say something racist. Maybe let the word 'nigga' slip out in the heat of an argument and solidify the strangle hold Democrats have on the black vote. And when it happens, when one of them slips up, people are going to know that he's said the word before or whatever. And that's exactly what I mean. See, if the Republicans know about these kinds of people in their own party, and do absolutely nothing about it, it just makes things worse for blacks. We just cling even tighter to a group of people who don't have our best interest at heart. We are still political footballs, being tossed to and fro, solidifying their power, and making us more dependent on them.

"So you think Sean Bellamy is going to do something different? He's going to change things, huh?"

"Well, he's planning to be a very radical president. One with ideas that would upset many political groups. Because of his revolutionary views on education, the military, the CIA, the IRS, Israel and the Palestinian situation, foreign policy, multiculturalism, drugs, and a host of other political minefields, he's hired a vast security force, which he plans to keep after he's elected. It's going to be interesting to watch."

"Keyth," I said in a relaxed tone.

"Yeah, baby."

"I love you."

"I love you, too."

"What would you say if I told you I'm late?"

"Late?"

"Late like I haven't had my period. I think you got me pregnant in California."

"So, you're not sure?"

"No, I'm not."

He smiled. "Well, let's make sure then," he said, and pulled my panties down.

# ABOUT THE AUTHOR

A native of Toledo, Ohio, Keith Lee Johnson
began writing purely by accident when a
literature professor unwittingly challenged
his ability to tell a credible story in class one day.
He picked up a pen that very day and has been
writing ever since. Upon graduating from high
school in June, Keith joined the United States
Air Force the following September and attained
a Top Secret security clearance. He served
his country in Texas, Mississippi, Nevada,
California, Turkey, and various other places
during his four years of service.
Keith has written four books and is currently
working on his fifth.

# AVAILABLE FROM
# STREBOR BOOKS INTERNATIONAL

**Baptiste, Michael**
*Cracked Dreams* 1-59309-035-8
*Godchild* 1-59309-044-7

**Bernard, D.V.**
*The Last Dream Before Dawn*
0-9711953-2-3
*God in the Image of Woman*
1-59309-019-6
*How to Kill Your Boyfriend (in 10 Easy Steps)* 1-59309-066-8

**Billingsley, ReShonda Tate**
*Help! I've Turned Into My Mother*
1-59309-050-1

**Brown, Laurinda D.**
*Fire & Brimstone* 1-59309-015-3
*UnderCover* 1-59309-030-7
*The Highest Price for Passion*
1-59309-053-6

**Cheekes, Shonda**
*Another Man's Wife* 1-59309-008-0
*Blackgentlemen.com* 0-9711953-8-2
*In the Midst of It All* 1-59309-058-2

**Cooper, William Fredrick**
*Six Days in January* 1-59309-017-X
*Sistergirls.com* 1-59309-004-8

**Crockett, Mark**
*Turkeystuffer* 0-9711953-3-1

**Daniels, J and Bacon, Shonell**
*Luvalwayz: The Opposite Sex and Relationships* 0-9711953-1-5
*Draw Me With Your Love*
1-59309-000-5

**Darden, J. Marie**
*Enemy Fields* 1-59309-023-4
*Finding Dignity* 1-59309-051-X

**De Leon, Michelle**
*Missed Conceptions* 1-59309-010-2
*Love to the Third* 1-59309-016-1
*Once Upon a Family Tree*
1-59309-028-5

**Faye, Cheryl**
*Be Careful What You Wish For*
1-59309-034-X

**Halima, Shelley**
*Azucar Moreno* 1-59309-032-3
*Los Morenos* 1-59309-049-8

**Handfield, Laurel**
*My Diet Starts Tomorrow*
1-59309-005-6
*Mirror Mirror* 1-59309-014-5

**Hayes, Lee**
*Passion Marks* 1-59309-006-4
*A Deeper Blue: Passion Marks II*
1-59309-047-1

**Hobbs, Allison**
*Pandora's Box* 1-59309-011-0
*Insatiable* 1-59309-031-5
*Dangerously in Love* 1-59309-048-X
*Double Dippin'* 1-59309-065-X

**Hurd, Jimmy**
*Turnaround* 1-59309-045-5
*Ice Dancer* 1-59309-062-5

**Johnson, Keith Lee**
*Sugar & Spice* 1-59309-013-7
*Pretenses* 1-59309-018-8
*Fate's Redemption* 1-59309-039-0

**Johnson, Rique**
*Love & Justice* 1-59309-002-1
*Whispers from a Troubled Heart*
1-59309-020-X
*Every Woman's Man* 1-59309-036-6
*Sistergirls.com* 1-59309-004-8

**Kai, Naleighna**
*Every Woman Needs a Wife*
1-59309-060-9

**Kinyua, Kimani**
*The Brotherhood of Man*
1-59309-064-1

**Lee, Darrien**
*All That and a Bag of Chips*
0-9711953-0-7
*Been There, Done That*
1-59309-001-3
*What Goes Around Comes Around*
1-59309-024-2
*When Hell Freezes Over*
1-59309-042-0
*Brotherly Love* 1-59309-061-7

**Luckett, Jonathan**
*Jasminium* 1-59309-007-2
*How Ya Livin'* 1-59309-025-0
*Dissolve* 1-59309-041-2

**McKinney, Tina Brooks**
*All That Drama* 1-59309-033-1

**Perkins, Suzetta L.**
*Behind the Veil* 1-59309-063-3

**Quartay, Nane**
*Feenin* 0-9711953-7-4
*The Badness* 1-59309-037-4

**Rivera, Jr., David**
*Harlem's Dragon* 1-59309-056-0

**Rivers, V. Anthony**
*Daughter by Spirit* 0-9674601-4-X
*Everybody Got Issues* 1-59309-003-X
*Sistergirls.com* 1-59309-004-8
*My Life is All I Have* 1-59309-057-9

**Roberts, J. Deotis**
*Roots of a Black Future*
0-9674601-6-6
*Christian Beliefs* 0-9674601-5-8

**Stephens, Sylvester**
*Our Time Has Come* 1-59309-026-9

**Turley II, Harold L.**
*Love's Game* 1-59309-029-3
*Confessions of a Lonely Soul*
1-59309-054-4

**Valentine, Michelle**
*Nyagra's Falls* 0-9711953-4-X

**White, A.J.**
*Ballad of a Ghetto Poet*
1-59309-009-9

**White, Franklin**
*Money for Good* 1-59309-012-9
1-59309-040-4 (trade)
*Potentially Yours* 1-59309-027-7

**Woodson, J.L.**
*Superwoman's Child* 1-59309-059-5

**Zane (Editor)**
*Breaking the Cycle* 1-59309-021-8